BAD FOR BUSINESS . . .

"Ain't seen you around Bannack before," Slocum's barber said, getting his implements of shaving and surgery ready.

"Been up above the Gulch for a month or more," Slocum said. "Lost my horse, and that slowed me down a mite." He leaned back in the chair and let the warm towel on his face soothe him even as it softened his wiry beard. The barber began stropping the razor, but with the slip-slip sound of steel against leather came another that brought Slocum upright in the chair. His hand flashed for the Colt Navy in its cross-draw holster.

Shots rang out before he could draw—but Slocum wasn't the target for the hail of lead. Three men had entered the barbershop, ringed the bearded man in the other chair, then opened fire on him without so much as a "how do you do." Their victim was cut to bloody ribbons before he could throw back the sheet covering his body. . . .

SLOCUM AND THE GOLD-MINE GAMBLE

JOVE BOOKS, NEW YORK

SLOCUM AND THE GOLD-MINE GAMBLE

A Jove Book / published by arrangement with
the author

PRINTING HISTORY
Jove edition / June 1996

The Putnam Berkley World Wide Web site address is
http://www.berkley.com

ISBN: 0-515-11878-8

A JOVE BOOK®
Jove Books are published by The Berkley Publishing Group,
200 Madison Avenue, New York, New York 10016.
JOVE and the "J" design are trademarks
belonging to Jove Publications, Inc.

PRINTED IN THE UNITED STATES OF AMERICA

10 9 8 7 6 5 4 3 2 1

1

John Slocum reached into his shirt pocket. All that rode there was a single rumpled greenback and a wad of lint that had slowly grown larger during the long Montana winter. He shrugged his broad shoulders and got his duster settled into place around his gaunt frame as he looked up and down the main street in Bannack. The warm Chinook wind that had kept him from freezing to death during the winter now tried to hide from him. Or was it simply the lack of money and prospects that chilled him so?

Slocum had been down on his luck before, but not like this. He had taken quite a tumble when his horse stepped in a gopher hole in mid-February. He had shot the Appaloosa and wished he could have shot himself. Though he had not broken his leg, he had pulled something loose in

1

his chest, making breathing difficult for the past two months.

He had holed up a couple dozen miles outside Bannack in the mountains, living off the land the best he could. It had taken the better part of two weeks to make his way into town after he felt up to it, and now he wasn't sure why he had bothered.

"One dollar," he grumbled to himself. That was all he had. One dollar. He stopped in front of a barbershop and smiled wryly as he studied his reflection in the large plate-glass window. In a mining boom town like Bannack the lone greenback was nowhere near enough to buy him a shot of whiskey in even the meanest of saloons or a decent meal in a café. But a haircut and shave might improve both his look and outlook.

"Howdy, mister," called the stout barber from the back of the store. "Come on in and set yourself down. I kin git to you right away."

"Much obliged," Slocum said, slinging his worn brown duster onto a convenient coat hook. He walked past the barber chair in the front of the store where another barber, a much younger, thinner man, worked on a customer with a full black beard and a nasty curl to his lip. Slocum didn't bother trying to make any pleasantries with that man. He had the look of someone who ate rattlesnakes for breakfast and rattled the rest of the day, just because he was so cussed. As Slocum had entered town, he had seen the ornery man riding past on the mare tethered outside and shouting curses at anyone who got in his path.

"Ain't seen you around Bannack before," Slocum's barber said, getting his implements of shaving and surgery ready.

"Been up above the Gulch for a month or more," Slocum said. He didn't mind the barber's chattering, but it riled him at the same time. He found himself both hungering for human contact and not liking it one bit.

"You're no miner, no, sir. I know 'em by their smell. All sweaty and stinkin' of Giant blasting powder. Alder Gulch is only for the hardrock miners and those danged greenhorns who don't know better."

"Lost my horse," Slocum said, "and that slowed me down a mite." He leaned back in the chair and let the warm towel on his face soothe him even as it softened his wiry beard. The barber began stropping the razor, but with the slip-slip sound of steel against leather came another that brought Slocum upright in the chair. His hand flashed for the Colt Navy in its cross-draw holster.

Shots rang out before he could draw—but Slocum wasn't the target for the hail of lead. Three men had entered the barbershop, ringed the bearded man in the other chair, then opened fire on him without so much as a "how do you do." Their victim was cut to bloody ribbons before he could throw back the sheet covering his body.

One of the murdering gunmen glanced in Slocum's direction, then dismissed him with a sneer, as if finding Slocum no threat. The three men holstered their six-guns and filed from the barbershop. Not a word had been spoken.

The entire while, Slocum's barber had continued stropping the razor as if nothing were wrong.

"Don't go movin' about on me now," the barber said, bending over his work. "No need to do unnecessary surgery on you."

"He's dead," Slocum said, staring at the man in the other chair. "Those varmints walked in, killed him, then sauntered out as sweet as you please."

"Reckon so," the barber said nonchalantly. To the other barber he called, "You get any blood on you, Jimbo?"

"No," Jimbo said, his voice shaky. "Not this time." Jimbo wiped sweat from his forehead, fished in a drawer for a bottle of rotgut, and took a long pull. He started to put the cork back in, then decided on a second shot. Slocum saw the man's hands shaking.

"This happen often?" Slocum had to ask.

"Often enough," the barber said, disgusted. "Wish they would do their business somewhere else."

"At least, they ought to have the good sense to do their killing closer to the undertaker's," Jimbo said. He pulled up the bloody sheet so it covered the bearded man's face. "Didn't even get paid for the work I done already."

"Now comes the bad part," muttered the barber as he smeared lather on Slocum's face. He paused for a moment when the sheriff and two deputies came into the shop. Like the killers before them, they said nothing. The two deputies grunted as they pulled the corpse from the chair and lugged it into the street.

"Morning, Sheriff Plummer," said Slocum's barber. "You needin' a shave today?"

"Not today. Maybe a bath and shave tomorrow, Ray."

"Whenever you like, a chair'll be waitin' for you," Ray said, applying the sharp edge of the razor to Slocum's face and beginning the shave. From the corner of his eye, Slocum watched Sheriff Plummer leave the shop, strolling off as if he were paying a Sunday visit to his best girl.

"This surely is a dangerous town," Slocum observed.

"Bannack's a mining town. Lots of poverty, a few rich miners, and a lot of busted dreams and gunplay," Ray explained as he worked. "That's not what this was about, though. It's them damned road agents. All the time shootin' up each other in their petty squabbles."

"It wouldn't be so bad," Jimbo cut in, "if they didn't take their feuds out into public. A few less of them thieves and we'd all be better off. But not the way they do it, shootin' up innocent people too."

Slocum lay back quietly in the chair, his mind working. What the barbers said sparked some interest. He was spending his last dollar on this shave. It seemed providential his future might be looking up as a result.

"Many gold shipments out of Bannack for them to rob?" he asked.

"Purty near every day," Ray said, flourishing the razor as he cut through the thicket of Slocum's beard. "That's why the road agents are thicker 'n flies on a cow-flop."

"What about that lawman? Sheriff Plummer, you called him. He looks equal to the chore of keeping robbers in fear of the law."

"Henry Plummer is a cold one, I'll give you that. He'd as like shoot you in the back as look at you when he's on a drunk. Sober, can't rightly say how good a sheriff he is. Bannack is pretty peaceful, except for the road agents and their deadly doings."

"Yeah," said Jimbo, "Bannack is quiet. It's out on the trail leading over to Boise and down into Utah where the real crime is."

Slocum didn't point out murder was usually a crime in most places. And in other places the sheriff would be madder than a wet hen that a man was cut down under his nose as the bearded outlaw had been. Most lawmen preferred their streets free of shooting and dead bodies. Henry Plummer seemed of a different bent.

"Here you go," Slocum said, handing Ray his solitary bill after finishing the haircut. The barber tucked the greenback into his pocket.

"Obliged, mister. Any time you need another shave—or even a bath—come on by. There's always room for a gentleman like you."

Slocum wondered at the barbershop's other customers, then glanced at the blood puddling on the seat of the other chair as he left. The wind turned warm again as he stepped into the Montana spring. He sucked in a deep breath and paused when his eyes lit on the saddled horse not ten paces away. It belonged to the dead man. The horse, a sturdy-looking dun mare, had been there when Slocum went inside the shop. He looked around a few minutes more, but saw no one likely to claim the horse. He went over and examined the horse.

"You and I will make quite a team," Slocum said. He fumbled in the saddlebags and found a roll of wanted posters from a half-dozen different towns, all bearing the general likeness of the bearded man with the sneer now likely on his way to the potter's field outside Bannack. Slocum had stashed his own gear outside town, not wanting to lug it in with him as he sized up Bannack.

He swung into the saddle, his long legs bent painfully. The stirrups would have to be adjusted, but that could wait for later. He didn't want people pointing him out as a horse thief—not before he got a chance at one of the gold shipments the barber had mentioned.

As he rode slowly from Bannack, Slocum's keen green eyes spied a heavy wagon being loaded with strongboxes from a local freight company office. It didn't take any imagination to picture the gold dust in each of those locked boxes. He walked his stolen mare past the straining driver and shotgun messenger, taking note of how they were armed and how likely they were to give up their cargo if confronted with a leveled six-shooter.

Slocum decided they had a worn look about them, telling of too little pay and too many risks. They wouldn't fight to keep the gold. As he rode out of Bannack, he was already thinking of it as *his* gold.

Slocum put his heels into the mare's flanks when he reached the edge of town. The number of deputies he spotted began to make him nervous. Sheriff Plummer might not bother guarding the gold shipments along the routes from Bannack, but he kept his men patrolling the town in pairs.

Riding faster once he was clear of the city limits, Slocum returned to where he had left his gear. His saddle wasn't as fine as the one on which he rode, but he decided to change anyway, to prevent anyone from recognizing the stolen gear. He checked his Winchester and then completely loaded his Colt. He usually rode with the hammer on an empty chamber to keep the ticklish rounds from going off while still in the holster.

Slocum figured he would need as much firepower as he could muster against the driver and his grizzled shotgun messenger.

Wasting no time, Slocum cut across a low ridge and worked his way south, in the direction most likely taken by the gold-laden wagon. He grinned when he heard the familiar clatter of steel-rimmed wheels against rock coming from over a low rise. Slocum urged the dun mare to a quicker pace, and reached the ridge in time to see the gold wagon rattling into view.

Slocum was no stranger to robbery, and knew this was a dangerous path he had started along. A single robber stood little chance against two armed and alert guards. From all he had heard in the barbershop, nobody drove this route without knowing how common it was for a band of road agents to hold up shipments destined for parts farther south.

He considered his chances at this rocky draw, and knew he would be buzzard bait if he tried. The shotgun-toting guard would see him coming from too far off. He had to find a place where he could work in close before springing his ambush.

Slocum turned his pony's face and got the balky mare trotting along the road, hunting for a spot giving both cover and surprise. As he rode Slocum felt the hairs on the back of his neck rise. During the war he had developed a sense about danger—not ignoring it had kept him alive through times where all those around him ended up in shallow graves.

Suddenly turning off the road eased the feeling somewhat. Slocum was still edgy and couldn't figure the reason. The best he could tell, nobody spied on him, though that was the likely cause of his discomfort. He headed across the rough, rocky terrain, picking his way between towering boulders. To his surprise, this led him back to the road.

"If that don't beat all," he said, seeing he had cut across a half mile of countryside rather than following a mile or more of meandering road through easier terrain. Slocum patted his horse's neck and eased the animal off the road and up a shale slope. The horse slipped and slid, but Slocum kept her moving until he reached the top of a rise giving him a good view of the road.

The road curved back into view not a hundred yards off. This allowed Slocum plenty of time to get back down the hillside and take cover behind any of a dozen boulders littering the area. He would rise, rifle on his shoulder, demand the driver stop, and within minutes be in possession of a ton of gold dust.

"Not a ton, but enough to keep me happy for a long, long time," he said, liking the notion he might be rich after all he had endured over the long winter. He spat, remembering the bitter roots he had lived on. The few scrawny rabbits that had graced his roasting spit would be replaced with juicy Delmonico steaks. And a new suit of clothes would be in order. The Montana winter and the rest of his travails had reduced his almost to rags.

Slocum cocked his head to one side, listening to the rumble of wagon wheels again. He levered a round into the chamber of his Winchester before starting down the slope to take his place alongside the road. Over and over he played through the robbery, as if he were watching a melodeon show and not taking part himself.

His horse would be safe enough on the hillside until he could get the wagon far enough down the road that the driver and guard would think he was going into the next county. He could fetch his horse, load all the gold he could into the saddlebags that had been filled with nothing more than the previous owner's peculiar vanity—Slocum had enough wanted posters drifting around with his name on them never to want to see another, much less collect the entire set—and then he would ride off to find a good place to spend his ill-gotten loot.

Simple. So simple.

And then the uneasiness returned. He chanced a quick look around the giant rock shielding him from view and saw nothing. Hands running up and down the length of his rifle in an unconscious gesture, he grew increasingly wary.

"Where's the wagon?" he wondered aloud. It ought to have been within range by now. Slocum rose, peering at the bend in the road as if willpower alone could force the gold-heavy wagon to appear. He was so keyed up, he jumped like a scalded dog when a gunshot rang out.

Slocum slid back behind the boulder, then realized the bullet hadn't come in his direction. The echo told him it came from around the bend—about where *his* gold shipment ought to be.

Knowing how foolhardy it was and not caring, Slocum ran into the middle of the road, jumping from one rut to the other to avoid muddy stretches. He slowed his headlong pace when he neared the bend in the road. He heard angry voices, followed by another shot.

"Goldang it, you don't hafta shoot us," came a complaining voice. "We done throwed down our guns."

"Get off that wagon," came a loud command. "You ain't goin' no farther in it."

"This is the third shipment I've lost this month," complained the driver. "The company's gonna fire my ass for sure."

"If you don't step lively, I'm gonna *shoot* your ass off before anybody has a chance to fire it."

Slocum pressed his back against a rocky wall and sidled around, rifle ready. He saw the driver drop to the ground. The shotgun messenger had already surrendered his weapon and stood off the road, looking fearful that the four men ringing the wagon might open fire at any instant. From the way they nervously fingered the triggers on the six-guns, Slocum knew how real that threat was.

They might be novice robbers, but they were taking *his* gold. He dropped to a crouch and considered his chances of shooting the four out of their saddles before they realized where the deadly barrage came from.

He immediately discarded such a notion when he saw he could never pick off more than one of the men due to the way they'd positioned themselves. Either clever planning or simple good fortune had placed them around the wagon so that he would find himself embroiled in a deadly firefight should he show himself now.

"Get that wagon moving," ordered the masked outlaw who seemed to be in charge. The only road agent Slocum had a clear shot at jumped from his horse into the driver's box. The outlaw grabbed up the reins, snapped them, and got the team moving.

Slocum dropped flat on the ground, letting the wagon rattle past. Before he could even think about bushwhacking the driver, the other three road agents galloped by, kicking up a choking cloud of dust. Slocum sputtered and wiped the grit from his eyes. By the time he got into the road, ready to fire, the wagon and four robbers were gone.

"I was right about one thing," he grumbled. "This was a good place for a robbery." The terrain he had intended to work for him now turned against him.

"Consarn it," came the peevish words from the direction of the robbery site. "Three shipments lost this month. The boss is gonna skin me alive. You too," the driver promised his guard.

"I ain't stayin' here one second longer," the guard declared. "I'm gonna sneak back into Bannack, then hightail it where they're not so organized."

"You call that organized?" protested the driver. "Well, let me tell you about the robbery I was in when . . ."

Slocum didn't stay to hear the tall tales of past thievery. He ran as hard as he could to get back to where his mare waited impatiently for him. Scrambling up the slope took precious minutes. And sliding his rifle into its sheath took more seconds.

He swung into the saddle, knowing he was a fool to try what he intended. But that gold was *his*, and he wasn't going to let any two-bit outlaws do him out of it.

Slocum was going to track them down and steal what, by rights, should have been his.

2

The road agents had a mile head start, but Slocum had no trouble following their trail. They drove along at a breakneck pace for less than ten minutes before the team tired, then proceeded at a more leisurely pace. As he followed, Slocum considered his chances of collecting an honest reward for capturing the outlaws and returning the gold—or simply taking the gold.

"Mine," he said to the mare, reaching down to pat the animal's neck. "I was robbed." The contorted logic did not bother him. Slocum felt Montana and the people in the territory owed him something for the long winter he had spent holed up in the mountains, minus a horse and not knowing if he was going to survive. The road agents working this route stole more gold than he ever would. A few paltry pounds of dust wouldn't be missed.

And Slocum would ride out to the coast, perhaps Seattle or somewhere in Oregon, using the gold to buy himself a string of sturdy Appaloosas that could be sold for good profit in California. It was his due.

The rattle of wagon wheels vanished, causing Slocum to worry he might have lost the robbers. He stopped to look at a narrow canyon branching off from the road. Slocum studied the rocky ground and decided the outlaws had finally left the road. Proceeding cautiously now that the way was turning close, Slocum dismounted and led his horse. The last thing he wanted was to blunder into the road agents' camp and have to shoot his way out.

A faint but still-visible track led up into the rocks. Slocum tethered his horse off the trail to where she would be hidden from casual discovery, and scrambled through the inanimate forest of rocks, his trusty Winchester ready for action. Atop a large, rough boulder he flopped belly down and studied the outlaws' camp.

Being cautious saved him from a deadly mistake.

Not only were the four robbers who had committed the theft in the bivouac, so were two others.

The leader from the robbery dismounted and went to where the pair stood off to one side. Whispered words were followed by an elaborate handshake, a secret identification guaranteeing they all belonged to the same gang. Such precautions surprised Slocum. It meant the four holding up the freight wagon didn't know the men taking the gold by sight. Otherwise, why go through the charade of identifying themselves as if they were traveling Freemasons?

Given the go-ahead by their leader after identification was made, the other three worked with military precision unloading the gold and placing it all into a pair of large strongboxes that they eventually slung over the back of a single pack burro.

"You did well," one of the newcomers told the road

agents' leader. "We will give you four an extra share to divvy up."

"That'll be appreciated," the robber said.

"Where'd you bury the driver and guard?"

This question caused the robbers' leader to bite his lower lip and look apprehensive. Slocum guessed the men were supposed to murder the two and had chickened out.

"Why do we have to wait till the end of the month?" complained one robber, breaking the tension and diverting attention from the location of two fresh graves. "This is like havin' a job and waitin' for wages to be paid out."

"We work this way because that's what you agreed to—and it's what the boss wants." The frosty words caused the four to exchange nervous glances. Mention of their leader put the thrill of fear into hardened crooks.

"Who is he anyway? All we saw was a guy with a black hood on his head."

The two laughed. "You don't want to know. We might have to kill you if you ever found out. Or worse. The boss might kill you himself—and he likes to watch men die real slow. Now get on out of here. We have a delivery to make."

With this dismissal, the four who had done the robbery abandoned the wagon in the middle of the campsite, went to their mounts, and retraced their path from the rendezvous.

"What do we tell the boss about them?" one of the remaining pair asked the other.

His companion shrugged. "They did all right, for their first job for us. But it was a cakewalk. We'll just report and let the boss worry about them." With that, the men mounted their own horses and led the burro deeper into the mountains.

Like a snake, Slocum slithered down the boulder and made his way to his horse. The four robbers had vanished already. He figured the fear of their unknown boss had lent

speed to their departure. Swinging into the saddle, Slocum
laid his rifle across his lap for easy use. Overtaking the
other two wouldn't be hard, not when they were leading a
gold-laden burro.

He followed the worn path back into the outlaw campsite. He frowned as he looked around. This was more than
a simple meeting spot. He jumped to the ground and studied
the scattered firepits. At least a dozen men had camped here
at one time—at the same time, if he was any kind of
tracker.

A glint off something in the dust caught his eye. He pried
it out of the hard-packed dirt and held it up. A Mexican
silver peso had been beaten into a deputy's badge.

Slocum knew many lawmen fancied such a gaudy display of wealth and power. But whoever had worn this one
was likely dead. A .44 slug had ripped out the center of
the badge, leaving only a jagged hole. Slocum ran his finger
around the bullet hole, then tossed it back to the ground.
A plugged peso wouldn't buy him anything, and the small
amount of silver wasn't worth the effort to save.

Not when he had a fortune in gold to collect.

He scouted the rest of the outlaws' camp before climbing
back into the saddle and heading up the canyon. The road
agents operated with clockwork precision, he decided. They
learned when the gold shipment was due, sent out one
group to rob the freighters, then another pair of outlaws
took possession of the booty. If the first group was caught,
which seemed unlikely, they wouldn't know where the gold
was.

And at the end of the month, as if they were simple
merchants pursuing their professions, they would be paid
off according to the risks they took.

Slocum let out a low whistle when he realized how powerful a gang he faced. They were well organized, showed
military discipline, and operated in secrecy. Even if all four
of the robbers were arrested, they could only identify the

two men they had handed the gold over to.

Slocum jerked back to the reality of his situation. The canyon walls were closing in on him, turning into little more than a crevice. Occasional glances at the hard-packed dirt floor convinced him he was still on the trail. But getting caught in this narrow passage would mean instant death if the men ahead discovered they were being followed.

Leaning to one side, Slocum pressed his ear against the rock wall. Distant echoes of hooves echoed back to him. The two still led their plodding burro on its slow, deliberate way back to camp.

Slocum maintained his pace until he came out of the tight passage. At one point his shoulders had brushed against either side of the crevice, but now he rode into a wide, grassy valley that stretched forever north and south. Staying in shadows, he squinted against the bright spring sun and tried to locate his quarry.

He found the two men and their burro meandering along a grassy path down to the valley floor, not ten minutes' hard ride ahead of him. But Slocum held back. They would spot him long minutes before he could overtake them.

"Time for a rest," he told the dun mare, patting her neck again. Slocum dismounted and rummaged through the saddlebags hunting for something more than old wanted posters. He found a bit of jerky and gnawed on it as he watched the two road agents head up the far side of the valley.

They did not hurry, but neither did the pair slow down. They rode as if intent on some specific destination. Slocum knew he had to get the gold before they arrived. He rubbed grit from his eyes, then shot to his feet when he tried to find them again and couldn't.

"They went into a canyon on the far side of the valley," he said in a low voice. His horse whinnied, as if saying this was the end of the ride.

It wasn't. Slocum could now gallop across the valley without fear of being seen. And he did. By the time he reached the far side of the valley, the mare was tuckered out and so was he.

A tiny stream provided water for the horse. He let her drink while he explored on foot. It took all his skill to find the exit used by the two outlaws. Any of a half-dozen different breaks in the wall surrounding the valley might have been taken—but one drew Slocum because of fresh spoor.

"No time to graze," he told his horse, pulling her from the stream bank. "We have to get the gold from those owl-hoots soon. These canyons are getting too complicated."

Riding after the robbers convinced him of that truth. Small canyons branched hither and yon, presenting a daunting array of choices for any posse tracking the robbers. Slocum found himself working harder and harder to keep on the right trail as the ground turned rockier with every step taken.

By late afternoon, Slocum had gotten himself turned around in the maze of towering rock spires and suddenly branching canyons, but he'd kept on the trail. He did not need to retrace his path after taking the gold from the two men. Simply riding toward the west would serve him well enough until he found the road to Coeur d'Alene.

Hearing horses whinnying and a burro braying, Slocum knew the pair had stopped for a spell. He wouldn't get a better chance to relieve them of their golden burden. Eyes peeled for any sign of a sentry in the rocks above him, Slocum rode ahead deliberately.

As he emerged from still another tight crevice in the rock, he caught his breath. Seldom had he seen such natural beauty. A valley tinged with the brilliant first colors of spring stretched over to a huge red monolith. A half-dozen freshets wandered down from the surrounding hills to merge near that brightly colored rock before turning to the east and streaming away in a respectable flow.

His quarry had dismounted near the red monolith and were brushing the trail dust from their clothing. One let his horse drink from a small stream while the other checked the cinches on the burro's load. Slocum knew it was time to act. If he let them continue on their way, he might lose them entirely in the gathering afternoon shadows. The towering vertical walls of rock turned day into twilight with startling rapidity.

Slocum tugged up his bandanna and settled it over his nose to hide his face. He might bluff his way close enough to bring his Winchester to bear on them if he pretended to be in their gang.

He put his heels into his mare's flanks and started down the slope, riding directly for the two road agents.

One looked up, pushed back his Stetson, scratched his head, and only then called to his partner. The man watering his horse glanced over his shoulder. Neither went for their six-shooters.

Slocum rode closer.

"Hey, what are you in such a big hurry for?" called the one who had first spotted Slocum.

"Got important news for the boss," Slocum shouted back, hoping this would set off another round of discussion and let him get even closer before they went for their guns.

"He's wearing a mask," said the other outlaw. "Why's he doing that? There's no dust gettin' kicked up, not on that grassland."

It was about this time both men realized Slocum was not one of their gang. And it was too late for them to do anything about it. Slocum lifted his rifle and got off a shot that knocked the one's dark Stetson into the air.

"Grab a handful of that fine blue Montana sky, gents," Slocum said. "I want what you have slung over the back of that burro."

"Do you know what you're doing?" asked the hatless man, more surprised than afraid. "You must have brass balls or be the world's dumbest jackass."

"Might be dumb," Slocum allowed, "but I'll be rich

and dumb. Move away from the burro.''

The two glanced at each other, as if sharing a huge joke. One even laughed, but they obeyed.

Slocum rode closer. It took only a few seconds to check the strongboxes slung over the burro's back. They both held the precious gold dust he had followed from Bannack. He caught up the trailing bridle of the burro and tugged gently to get it moving.

''You got any last words, mister?'' asked the outlaw as he reached down and brushed off his hat. He ran a finger into the hole through the brim Slocum had just put there and shook his head sadly before looking back at his attacker.

The hair on the back of Slocum's neck rose, warning him he had made a terrible mistake. Neither of the men went for their six-guns. They didn't have to, not with a dozen men armed with rifles on top of the red rock monolith and coming around from a hidden camp.

Slocum found himself staring down the bores of enough rifles to put him six feet under in a flash.

3

"What's going on here?" asked one of the men with his rifle leveled. The frown on his face told how confused he was at seeing three men instead of two with the gold.

"I caught them trying to steal the shipment," Slocum shouted, intending to spread as much confusion as possible. "The boss isn't going to like it if we lose the gold."

"What?" cried the outlaw closest to the burro. "Me and—"

Slocum never let him get any farther. He fired his rifle and caught the man in the shoulder, spinning him around. The man's arms flew outward and as his hands came down, they slapped hard on the burro's rump. The animal brayed loudly, reared, and bolted, running as fast as any quarter horse in a claiming race.

Taking advantage of the confusion, Slocum got off a

couple more shots. He didn't fire his rifle as much to kill or wound as to create even more chaos. It worked. The shrill protests of the remaining road agent who had brought the gold into the camp by the red rock monolith were drowned out in the hubbub. Although many rifles were still aimed in his direction, Slocum took another chance and put his heels into his mare's heaving flanks.

The horse shot forth, frightened and running hard after the still-fleeing burro laden with the stolen gold dust. As Slocum blasted past a knot of the outlaws, he saw how heavily armed they were. Most had two six-shooters shoved into their belts or hanging at their sides in holsters. Many had Arkansas toothpicks shoved into boot sheaths, and all were sporting shotguns or rifles.

"Hey, wait, we don't know you!" shouted one road agent as Slocum raced past him. "You gotta give the password or secret handshake!"

Slocum kicked hard, knocking away the man's shotgun. It discharged with a thunder that deafened Slocum and knocked back the bandit. The man sat heavily in the dirt, the deadly weapon slithering away from his grip.

Slocum put his weight forward on the horse's shoulders and urged the mare to jump. He cleared the downed man and found himself on the far side of the monolith, shielded from the body of road agents by a few of their number. If they wanted to kill the interloper, they had to take out a few of their partners to do it.

He heard loud shouts of rage as everyone began firing as one. A few slugs whined past his head, but Slocum stayed low and kept the horse at a dead gallop. In minutes, the horse began to flag and Slocum eased back on his headlong retreat.

"Keep going, old girl. Don't fail me now," he urged the mare. Slocum had no idea if the horse's previous owner had mistreated her, but the animal responded in the worst way possible. The mare straightened her front legs, lowered her head, and tried to throw him. Slocum's reflexes saved him from taking a tumble that would have meant his death.

In spite of the confusion reigning supreme behind him, some order was returning. The road agents would be finding their mounts and coming after him in jig time. If he landed on the ground flat on his back, he would be buzzard bait in minutes.

"All right, no running," Slocum said to the horse. She turned a huge white-rimmed brown eye in his direction, as if appraising his honesty. The mare snorted and let Slocum coax her into a trot, following the burro into a side canyon.

Slocum knew he had little chance of getting all the gold from the burro and escaping with such a load. The cries behind him were taking more form. Whoever commanded the outlaw band had regained control and formed a posse intent on cutting Slocum's throat from ear to ear.

"This way, come on, old girl," he implored the horse. Slocum heaved a sigh of relief when the horse obeyed. They followed the burro down a dusty, winding trail that quickly petered out. The burro stopped and looked around, exhausted from its run and confused about where to go.

Slocum hit the ground and ran to the burro. He heaved one strongbox from the cargo sling and dropped it to the ground. The burro reared and stumbled, then resumed its headlong flight. Slocum would have swatted its rump again to get it moving, if he had been close enough. The burro provided a diversion he would sorely need.

Using the butt of his rifle, he knocked off the padlock and threw open the strongbox. Inside lay two large bags of gold dust. Slocum grabbed one and got it into the right saddlebag. It took only a few seconds longer to transfer the other bag of dust into the left saddlebag, giving the horse a more even load to struggle under.

The horse neighed in protest. Slocum didn't immediately mount, preferring to lead the horse away into still another rocky crevice. He saw some signs this wasn't a dead end.

If it had been, he would have been trapped like a rat.

Slocum heaved a sigh of relief when the narrow crack in the rock opened to a tall-walled canyon. It felt as if he had spent half his life struggling through the crevice. As he came into the canyon, sparse as it was with only spots of vegetation here and there, it felt as if he had entered an earthly paradise.

"You rested?" Slocum asked the horse. The mare glared at him. She wanted water. She wanted food. Most of all, she wanted rest. Slocum knew there would be none of those forthcoming unless they got far away from the road agents. He could make a stand at the mouth of the crevice, taking potshots at the men as they filed out.

He could, but he knew better. There had to be a way around this narrow passage—and the outlaws would know it. Besides, Slocum didn't have enough ammo to hold off an army of determined, angry outlaws.

He had stolen their booty from under their noses. Even if they never saw the gold, they would hunt him down for revenge.

Dropping to one knee, Slocum yanked hard at stumps of scrubby brush seemingly growing from solid rock. He twisted and tugged until the roots broke free. Then, using strips torn from his bandanna, he tied the brush to the horse's hind legs. The mare tried crow-hopping to avoid this further indignity, but Slocum would have none of it.

"We need it to hide our trail," he said, wishing he had a lariat. That would make dragging the brush easier. But he didn't and had to make do with what he had.

He swung into the saddle and got the mare moving at a canter for a few hundred yards, then dropped to a slow walk, moving into a trot to vary the pace and give the horse a chance to regain her wind. The brush made swish-swish sounds that Slocum knew would carry along the narrow canyon. He immediately took the right fork when he came to a branching valley.

He began to feel pretty good about his boldness in snatching the gold from under the noses of the outlaws. Not realizing he had ridden into their main camp had been a terrible mistake, but he had come out all right in the end. He glanced over his shoulder at the bulging saddlebags filled with enough gold dust to keep him in whiskey and good smokes for a long, long time.

"Not enough for a real remuda," he decided, "but it is a good start. A poker game or two where they don't know the odds and—"

He bit off his self-congratulation when he heard sounds from ahead. Horses. Men yelling. He dropped from the back of the mare and fought to keep her from bolting. She wanted nothing more than to be away from the rider who forced her to bear not only his weight but that of the stolen gold.

Slocum tugged hard on the bridle and got the mare moving through tangled bramble bushes. The sharp thorns cut at his body and legs; Slocum never noticed. He was too busy trying to find cover. Seconds after he entered a small stand of lodgepole pines, he heard heavy thudding of horses' hooves from up the valley.

With his hand over the mare's nostrils to keep her quiet, Slocum peered out from his meager cover. Outlaws, each and every one. He didn't know if they had been among those at the red monolith, and it did not really matter.

If they caught any stranger trespassing on their territory, they wouldn't take kindly to it. Slocum knew they would shoot first and never bothering asking questions at all.

"He didn't come this way. Jed's full of it," the lead rider grumbled. "We should have stayed on the burro's trail. I don't trust the others not to take a few ounces of dust for themselves and claim that varmint stole it."

"He got clean away," said the second outlaw. "I never seen anything like it in all my born days."

"I did," the leader said. "It was back in Laramie. This

mangy cayuse from the Cimarron Strip come along and . . ." The men's voices trailed off as they crossed the terrain Slocum had already covered. He let out a deep breath he hadn't known he was holding when he saw the four riders had disappeared down the narrow valley.

Mind racing, Slocum tried to figure out his best escape route. If he kept going, in the direction the riders had approached from, he might run into more of them. But following would be suicidal. Sooner or later, they would look back and see him on their trail.

He had gotten turned around in the deep canyons, and took a few minutes to get his bearings. The sun had dipped far below the rim, casting twilight throughout the maze of rocky byways. Slocum had to keep moving or they would find him for sure. Only a good, long distance between him and the road agents would let him rest easy.

He led his horse to one rocky wall of the valley and followed the sheer stone for almost a mile before finding a branching trail. Slocum had no idea where it led and it didn't much matter to him. The darkness was almost complete, but deliberately kept him and his horse from stepping into a gopher hole.

Slocum had been that route once this year. He wasn't about to be put on foot again owing to another busted horse leg.

He was so intent on not stumbling about and making noise he did not see the man with the leveled six-gun ahead of him.

"Hold it right there," came the cold command. Slocum's head jerked up. In the faint illumination cast from reflected sunset he saw light glinting off the outlaw's six-shooter.

"Glad I found you," Slocum said immediately, thinking he might bluff his way to freedom again. "I—"

"You nothing," the man snapped. "You're the bushwhacking son of a bitch we're all looking for. Get those hands of yours raised real high."

When the man gestured with his six-shooter, Slocum took the only chance he had. The road agent jerked his gun skyward in the direction he expected Slocum's hands to travel. His aim was off when he saw Slocum move in the opposite direction.

A foot-long tongue of orange and yellow flame erupted from the man's six-gun, but the slug went high and to Slocum's left. The gunman didn't get a second chance. Slocum cleared leather and his first shot caught the outlaw smack in the center of his belly. The man grunted, doubled over, and folded like a pocket knife.

Slocum put a second shot into the dark mass crumpled on the ground, just to be sure. He had already drawn attention to himself by the gunfire. He didn't need to leave an outlaw behind him, wounded and willing to backshoot him.

"What's goin' on?" came a loud shout from Slocum's left.

"Rattlers," Slocum replied. "A whole nest of them." As he spoke he led his mare to the right.

"You need any help, Garth?"

"No," Slocum shouted back. The instant he had spoken he knew he had made a mistake. The creaking of saddle leather told him three or more men were mounting, ready to come after him. The dead guard's name probably wasn't Garth and this was the road agent's way of identifying his guards.

Slocum swung into the saddle, felt the mare sag under his weight, and knew he could never come out ahead in any race. He still had to try. He got the horse moving along at a brisk walk, barely able to pick her way in the darkness.

As he rode Slocum hunted for a place to hole up. He didn't see any.

Boldness had kept him alive this long. He had to try something daring again or he wouldn't see the sunrise. Circling and trying to double back, he ran smack dab into another band of riders.

For a moment, they stared at each other, Slocum at the five road agents and them at him.

Then all hell broke loose.

Shotguns blasted. Rifles cracked. Six-shooters chimed in with their deadly voices.

Slocum ducked low and spun about. His frightened horse put on a burst of speed that quickly died. He knew the valiant mare was on her last legs. He had asked for too much from the animal and now he had to pay.

"There he is. Ahead! Get him, men. Fill him full of holes!"

More lead sang through the night, kicking up dust all around Slocum. He got his mare behind a boulder, giving partial shelter. But he saw immediately he wouldn't walk away unscathed. Riders from behind were galloping toward him, and he faced five men in front of him.

Then an idea formed that was as dangerous as it was daring. Slocum grabbed his rifle and jumped from behind the boulder. He opened up on the men who had blocked his retreat. After he had emptied his rifle's magazine, he whipped around, drew his six-shooter, and fired the remaining shots at the outlaws riding down on him from behind.

Rifle and Colt empty, Slocum dived back into the shelter of the tumble of rocks. The shotgun blasts and rifle reports had been deafening before. Now they threatened to burst his eardrums.

As the two groups of outlaws shot at each other in the dark, Slocum frantically reloaded his rifle and Colt Navy. As the fire died down, he emptied both his weapons again to get the road agents riled and willing to shoot at any moving in the night.

"I got 'im!" came the triumphant shout. "I plugged him!" The exultant cry was cut off in a bloody burbling as a returning bullet stole the man's life.

New volleys were fired. Then finally someone caught on to what Slocum had done.

"Hold yer fire, dammit! Everyone, hold yer fire! We're gunnin' down one another. That varmint might have high-tailed it!"

A few rounds were discharged after the order to cease fire, but Slocum was again impressed—and worried—by the ready obedience of the road agents. They had been well trained, and that spoke ill of his chance to escape.

"Who got plugged?" A solitary man strode out from a rocky sanctuary, confident Slocum would not cut him down. Even more amazing, he had no fear of being shot by his own men. "Drag the bastard out here and let's tend to him. And find the gold!"

Slocum knew he had little time to waste. The firefight he had tried to get going had fizzled out like a wet fire-cracker. He grabbed his horse's reins and started to mount. There had to be another way to escape this trap.

He quickly saw the horse wasn't going to budge. She had shown a stubborn streak earlier. Now she simply stood, as if daring him to do his worst.

The sounds of the road agents getting organized to come after him decided Slocum. He could never get clean away on the mare and with the gold. A quick look at the horse told him she had reached the end of her ride for the day.

But she might still get him out of this fix.

Slocum whipped out his knife and drove the blade deep into the saddlebags on either side. A tiny trickle of gold dust filtered out. He scooped up a few grains and put them into his pocket where they joined the lint in a comforting lump.

Then he placed his rifle barrel against the horse's rump and fired.

The suddenly hot barrel caused the horse to neigh loudly and race off.

Slocum ducked down as the cries rose.

"There he goes. After him!"

Slocum watched as the outlaws charged past his hiding place, intent only on the horse. When their leader saw traces of the gold dust on the trail, this spurred all the outlaws to even harder riding.

For the moment, John Slocum was left alone and on foot. He had to make the best of his chance if he wanted to get away with his hide in one piece. He started walking fast, going away from the direction chosen by his frightened horse.

4

"Fifty dollars to the man who finds him," came the chilling offer. Slocum huddled in the crevice of rocks crushing him on either side, watching intently as four road agents rode past his hiding place. He didn't know which of the owl-hoots made the offer, but he knew it was a worthwhile bounty for a few minutes' work.

The number of men hunting him down had increased as the night wore on.

Letting the mare run off trailing gold dust behind had given Slocum enough of a head start to evade the outlaws, but on foot he was at a distinct disadvantage. Faced with dozens of the bloodthirsty, money-hungry bounty hunters, he eventually would be flushed out unless he did something daring.

Slocum chuckled at the idea. He had been doing nothing

but taking huge risks since going after the gold shipment. And so far, those gambles had paid off. He touched the gold dust in his shirt pocket. The problem was that the risks hadn't paid off enough.

Then two riders came back up the trail.

"The boss isn't gonna like this, Hunter."

"Shut up, Buck," was the acid reply. "He doesn't need to know we let that varmint get away." The one named Hunter raised his voice and shouted loud enough to send echoes down the canyon. "A hundred dollars! I'm offering a hundred in gold if you bring him in before midnight!"

"You ought to let the boss know, Hunter," muttered Buck.

Slocum struggled to get a good look at the two men. Names flowed like a fast-running stream in Montana. Hunter and Buck might be summer names, but it gave Slocum something to be on the lookout for later. After he got away.

If he got away.

The two outlaws rode slowly along the canyon trail, giving Slocum a clear shot at their backs. His finger drummed on the trigger of his Winchester. He had the ammo and he had the skill to kill two road agents. Slocum held back, not knowing where the others searching for him might be. If he could have killed one and stolen his horse, he would have taken the chance. But against two? He wasn't going to take needless risk.

After the pair disappeared into the gloom, Slocum pushed free of the narrow crack where he had wedged himself. Looking up, he saw the jagged canyon rim two hundred feet away blocking out some of the brilliant stars in springtime constellations. He heaved a sigh and knew where he had to go if he wanted to escape.

Slocum began climbing. By midnight he had reached the rim and cheated some outlaw of his hundred-dollar reward. He peered down into the maze of canyons and shook his head. Getting away from the outlaws would have been difficult down there, if not impossible. They knew intimately the byways afforded by the spiderweb of rocky gorges. Slocum wished one or two of the road agents would show himself so he could potshot them, as he had done in the war as a sniper for the Confederacy, but nothing moved to give him a decent target.

Rifle hiked up over his shoulder as if marching in formation, he located the North Star, got his bearings, and then set off to find the main road leading into Bannack. A little after sunrise, footsore and every bone in his body aching, Slocum reached the twin-rutted road.

He considered heading on to Helena or even starting for the coast. Slocum knew he wouldn't get too far, not with the road agents working every inch of this dusty turnpike. Better to go back to Bannack, get another horse, and then leave the territory pronto.

He touched the few grains of gold in his pocket and wondered if it would be enough to buy a horse. He doubted it, but he might find a card game in some saloon. There a few glittering specks might turn into a pile of nuggets.

No sooner had Slocum started hoofing it toward the boom town than he heard loud cursing from around a bend in the road. He took the rifle from his shoulder and got off the road, working forward slowly to be sure he wasn't walking into a hornet's nest of outlaws.

His eyes widened when he saw two people standing next to a carriage with one wheel leaning at an angle. The axle might have broken or the nut simply come loose. But the two held his attention, fully, especially the woman.

The man was tall, slender, and had the look of a dandy about him. Tiny puffs of white lace poked out at his cuffs and a brocade jacket gleamed in the morning sun. Slocum ignored the man to stare at the lovely woman with him.

She came to the man's shoulder and was elaborately dressed. The bodice of her dress was pleasantly full, her waist trim, and her hips flaring. As she turned, Slocum saw evidence of a bustle waggling about delightfully. Whether he betrayed himself or she had some sixth sense, Slocum could not tell.

The woman turned and stared at him directly. Her long, dark hair fell over one shoulder in a lustrous stream caught lightly by the morning breeze. Her eyes were deep blue and piercing, intelligence and wit shining forth. In his day Slocum had seen pretty women, but no one this beautiful.

He heaved a sigh. Beautiful hardly did her justice. Gorgeous.

And what was she doing with that fop who turned and also stared at Slocum, after taking a lace handkerchief from his vest pocket, disturbing a dangling golden chain in the process?

Slocum got to his feet and lowered his rifle. There was no danger from these two.

"I say, you ruffian, why are you spying upon us in that uncouth manner?" The man waved the handkerchief in Slocum's direction.

"Didn't mean to spy. I heard somebody cussing and came to see what was wrong." Slocum recoiled slightly when he saw the man wore makeup like a painted whore.

The woman wore only a touch of rouge on her cheeks and some artfully applied lipstick to enhance the fullness of her lips. Slocum reckoned the woman could give her companion some advice.

"Oh, yes, Lord Benbow does have a temper," she said. Slocum thought of soft wind blowing through tall pines on a summer evening when she spoke.

"Lord Benbow?" He pulled his eyes off her and back to the man. The man performed an elaborate bow.

"Allow me to present myself, good sir. I am Samuel, Lord Benbow. And this dear lady is my wife, the Lady Benbow."

"Gloria, please call me Gloria," she said, holding her hand out. Slocum wasn't quite sure what he was supposed to do. He took it and started to shake it, then took her subtle hint and leaned over to kiss her hand.

"This is most refreshing, my dear," Benbow said. "A barbarian with a touch of civilization about him. And he has a pleasant accent also. I say, sir, are you one of those ruffians from Texas?"

"Georgia," Slocum said, not wanting to get into a long recitation of his background. For the Englishman it would be both amusing and horrifying.

"Ah, the South. Little wonder he shows signs of civility. I have always said Southern gentlemen are among the finest in the world," Gloria Benbow replied, her smile brighter than the rising sun.

"If you need help, I might be able to fix your carriage." Slocum dragged his eyes away from Gloria's beauty and studied the axle. It was a mite bent, but the real culprit was as he had thought. The nut had come loose, letting the wheel slip off.

"We would be forever indebted to you, sir," Lord Benbow exclaimed.

Slocum scouted around and found the nut a few yards back down the road. He came back and handed the nut to Benbow.

"When I lift the carriage and get the wheel into position, thread the nut back on."

"Oh." Benbow held the nut as if it might bite him.

Slocum bent down, got a good grip, then lifted. The carriage was not as heavy as he thought, from the way it was loaded with trunks and travel cases. He wiggled the wheel back into place and then motioned for Benbow to spin the nut on. To Slocum's surprise, the man did the job right the first time. Benbow stepped back and dusted off his hands, smiling broadly.

"I say, I have fixed this balky conveyance! Imagine the stories we shall have to tell the Queen!"

"The Queen?" asked Slocum.

"Queen Victoria, of course," Gloria said. Her lips parted slightly and the tip of her tongue slipped out to make a slow circuit in a suggestive manner. Slocum wasn't sure, but he thought Gloria thrust out her chest just a bit more to show off her breasts to him.

"Come, my dear, let us get on into this boomtown, I think it is called. Is that correct, sir?" Samuel Benbow looked to Slocum for confirmation.

"About ten miles down the road."

"Samuel, I have an idea. Why not hire Mr. . . . ."

"Slocum, John Slocum," he supplied.

"Why not hire Mr. Slocum as a guide? He has shown himself to be quite useful. And he appears to know how to use that formidable weapon of his."

Slocum swallowed when he saw Gloria's eyes weren't on his rifle but on his crotch. She was a bold one, especially in front of her husband.

"Capital idea. Yes, Mr. Slocum, was it? Mr. Slocum, will you act as our guide as we explore this primitive frontier? We cannot offer much, not more than, say, fifty dollars a week. Would that be enough?"

Slocum blinked at such a large sum. He would have been willing to show them around for the price of a good horse and tack.

Gloria spoke up. "See, my darling, I told you prices were much higher out here. Perhaps Mr. Slocum might consider our offer for fifty dollars and a horse." She clung to Samuel Benbow's arm, but her eyes bored into Slocum's.

"I had to put my horse down when he stepped into a gopher hole and broke a leg," Slocum said. He saw no reason to mention the mare he had stolen from a dead man.

"We can aid one another then. Come, can you drive this rig?"

"I can try," Slocum said. He climbed into the carriage and took the reins. The horse strained to get the laden carriage moving. All the way into Bannack, Slocum rode with his hip pressed firmly against Gloria's warm leg—and with her hand resting on his upper thigh.

"Oh, look at the antediluvian structures," crowed Samuel Benbow as they drove into town. "Simply fabulous. The stories we will have to tell when we return to England!"

"Where can we stay?" asked Gloria, her hand squeezing down lightly on Slocum's leg.

"Reckon there's one or two hotels that would suit folks of your station," Slocum said. He stopped in front of the Royal Hotel. It was a two-story brick structure and looked to be in the best repair of any of the hotels along Bannack's main street.

"This looks far superior to the other establishments where we have stayed," Benbow said, climbing down. He went around the carriage and up onto the veranda, putting hands on his hips to survey the new sights.

Slocum got out and helped Gloria down from the carriage. His hands lingered a moment longer than proper on her slim waist. She didn't seem to mind. If anything, she moved a bit closer to him, rubbing her breasts against him.

"Please arrange for two rooms, will you, my good man?" called Benbow.

"Two?"

"Why, yes, of course. One for Lady Benbow and me, another for yourself. I will not have my servants wandering off in the middle of the night. If you are to show us every nook and cranny of this tedious, dangerous land, you must stay close by."

"Don't take him too seriously," Gloria said in a whisper, when Slocum bristled at being called a servant. "For my sake, please do as he says."

"Very well," Slocum said. As he climbed the steps, Benbow turned and thrust a thick wad of greenbacks at him.

"Here, my good man. Rent the rooms for us, then replenish our supplies for a lengthy—what do you call it?—

for a scout tomorrow. A picnic lunch would be adequate, I think, if you can find a decent wine to accompany the viands.''

With that, Benbow took his wife's arm and started off down the street.

"Get the trunks into our room while we explore this marvelously uncivilized boom town. A boom town, imagine that, my dear.''

"Yes, my darling," Gloria said, but she turned so she could shoot Slocum another of her hot looks.

How such cold blue eyes could carry such a hint of passion was beyond Slocum's understanding. For all that, why a hot-blooded woman like Gloria Benbow had married such a vain dandy made his head ache with the effort of figuring it out. Slocum tucked the thick wad of bills into his pocket, no longer caring about the few grains of gold dust there, and went to rent the rooms.

After he lugged up the trunks, put the horse and carriage into the local livery, and purchased another sturdy saddle horse and gear for himself, Slocum decided it was time to find his employers. Slocum always gave his boss a full day's work, even if he worked for a popinjay like Samuel, Lord Benbow.

And, Slocum had to admit, he wanted to see Gloria again. How long he would work for them was a question he could not easily answer. Their money was a strong factor, but the threat of the road agents might drive him out of the territory sooner than he wanted.

Slocum found the Benbows had left behind a wake of laughter and bawdy comments as they made their way into Bannack's roughest section of town. He stopped outside the Poled Ox dance hall and peered inside. A crowd clustered around a table, chuckling at the show going on.

Slocum pushed through the swinging doors and made his way to one side where he got a better view of the entertainment. His eyes widened. Sitting beside Lord Benbow was his wife. To bring a lady into such an establishment branded her as a whore. Slocum wondered if Benbow knew that—or if Gloria cared.

"So I said to this huge brute, 'Why are you not wearing proper silk stockings?' " cried Benbow. The crowd of miners roared in amusement, but Slocum knew they were laughing at the Englishman, not with him.

"Lord, your room's ready," Slocum said, hoping to get the man out of the dance hall before trouble began.

"I am having a capital time, Mr. Slocum. Why not show my dear wife back to our suite? I'll be along later, after I've purchased drinks for all my new friends!"

The loud roar of approval that rose drowned out Slocum's protests. Gloria rose and gripped his arm. He knew better than to argue with the man paying his wages. If Benbow wanted to buy drinks for the bottomlessly thirsty miners, it was his money to waste.

Outside, Slocum said, "Do you know that only loose women go into such places?" He tipped his head back in the direction of the dance hall.

"Why, no, but I suspected," Gloria said. "The only women we've seen in such places were, how do you call them? Soiled doves? Cyprians?"

"Whores," Slocum said, hoping to shock some sense into her. Gloria only laughed. At the lovely sound Slocum's anger faded.

"You really are looking out for our well-being, aren't you?"

"Reckon so. Even if I wasn't paid to do it, I would," Slocum said. "I'm not sure why you are exploring the West, but it *is* a dangerous place unless you know what you're doing."

"Going into saloons and gambling parlors isn't on your list of recommended activities for a lady?" Slocum heard the teasing tone Gloria used.

"Something like that."

"Let me explain our dalliance in this primitive land, Mr. Slocum," Gloria said. "Lord Benbow is fabulously wealthy, and with such riches comes boredom. He heard of the adventure to be found on your Western frontier and decided to sample it firsthand. We have been roaming about for a month or so, trying to find this adventure, and it is proving elusive."

"You're lucky you weren't robbed on the way into Bannack," he told her. "The road is filthy with road agents. They seem well organized," he said.

"Ah, yes, we have heard of them. An amazing organization."

"How's that?" Slocum frowned. He hadn't expected Gloria to know the first thing about such . . . ruffians.

"They have couriers that maintain contact from one town to another, are organized like a military company with captains and lieutenants and sergeants, and it is even rumored they mark promising targets with secret symbols. Troopers posted along the roadway relay information and organize robberies." Gloria paused for a breath of air. A blush had come to her cheeks as she was visibly excited by the prospect of such an outlaw band.

"You know more about them than I do," Slocum said slowly. "Still, you and your husband rode along the road, daring them to rob you?"

"Quite an experience that would be," she said. Gloria tossed her head like a frisky filly and sent back a banner of raven's-wing dark hair. The evening breeze caught it and fluttered it like a banner.

"I don't understand you," Slocum said, shaking his head.

"My need for adventure or marrying Samuel?" Her blue eyes fixed on him, daring him to respond.

"Both, either," Slocum admitted.

"We enjoy being mysterious," Gloria said. "I feel it is time to turn in."

Slocum nodded, opening the door leading into the Royal Hotel lobby for her. She slid past, again rubbing lightly against his body. Slocum took a deep breath and let it out slowly. Gloria did not bother looking back as she climbed the stairs and vanished down the corridor, going into her room.

Hers and her husband's.

Slocum nodded to the room clerk, then climbed the stairs and went to his room. It would be nice having a mattress under him for the first time in long months. Even with a decent blanket, the ground got hard mighty quick.

Hanging up his gun belt and shucking off his boots, Slocum stretched out on the bed, staring at the cracks in the plastered ceiling. Lack of sleep stole away his intention to think through working for Lord and Lady Benbow. In seconds he slept.

And John Slocum came immediately awake almost an hour later when he heard the door to his room opening on its creaking hinges. He sat bolt upright and reached for his Colt Navy—until he saw the heavenly figure silhouetted in the doorway.

Gloria Benbow slipped into the room like a ghost and sat on the bed next to him. The pale light filtering in the room window turned her into an angel, a scantily clad angel.

"What are you doing here?" he asked.

"I waited for you. When you didn't come, I decided to see why. You had actually fallen asleep in this lumpy bed." She bounced up and down on the mattress, moving closer. "I know many more interesting things to do in a bed."

"Your husband," Slocum protested. He wasn't about to cuckold any man, even a dandy like Samuel Benbow.

He had no chance to further his protest. As her full red lips crushed into his, all Slocum's resolve fled. His arms circled her lithe body and pulled her closer. He felt the hardness of her nipples through the thin nightgown she wore and the pulsing of her heart as passions mounted.

Leaning back, Slocum pulled her down on top of him. The kiss changed subtly as his lips parted. Gloria's tongue darted out snakelike and teased his. Before he could reply in kind, she pulled her mouth from his and began kissing his face, his neck, and lower. As she did, she unfastened his shirt and unbuttoned his pants.

"Oh," she said in a small but delighted voice as his erection sprang forth.

"It's been like that ever since I saw you out on the road," Slocum allowed.

"You poor thing. Let's do something special for this poor, long-suffering prisoner."

Slocum gasped as Gloria's lips closed on the very tip of his manhood. The tongue that had delighted his, now performed a miracle. It made him even harder. But Gloria wasn't satisfied with sampling him—and this suited Slocum just fine.

As Gloria climbed over him, as if mounting a horse, he reached out and brushed aside the silky nightgown. Two mounds of firm breast filled his palms. He squeezed. Gloria tossed her head back and closed her eyes. She sighed in sheer pleasure at the way he fondled her.

His fingers found the coppery tips and squeezed down on them. The woman's heart pounded out excited blood into those fleshy nubbins until they were as hard as Slocum.

"No more," she sobbed. "I can't stand this. I need you in me, John. Inside me!" She pushed more of her nightgown out of the way, and moonlight bathed her naked body.

Silvery and totally exposed to his lustful gaze, Gloria writhed sensuously like a snake. Her dark hair flowed around her shoulders, hiding her ample breasts in one moment and then exposing them the next. But as much as Slocum loved the feel of her silken flesh under his fingers, he liked the way her tight channel totally engulfed him.

Rising and then dropping, she took him full length into her. The tight, damp tunnel constricted around him, as if she meant to squeeze him to death. But what a death that would be!

Before Slocum could even protest such a fate, Gloria rose slowly. His long shaft slid easily from her until only the purpled tip remained within her nether lips. She simply relaxed and came plummeting down. Over and over she did this, grinding her crotch into his.

Then Slocum could not stand being passive any longer. The feel was superb around his turgid length, but he wanted more. He sat up, and his arms circled her.

"Let me get my legs straightened," she said hotly in his ear. As she spoke she nibbled, inflaming him even more.

With her legs thrust out on either side of his body and Slocum's stiffness still within her, they kissed and fondled one another until Slocum found himself trying to lift her entirely off the bed.

"Yes, John," she said, eyes bright with lust. "Do it now. Make me burn inside!"

He leaned forward and got his knees under him. Her legs parted even more to his gentle invasions. Slowly at first, then building speed and power with every stroke, he drove squarely into her intimate center. Gloria began moaning and thrashing about. Slocum moved faster. His entire length came alive, tingling and sending pleasure washing throughout his loins.

When he thought he could no longer stand the pace, Gloria let out a shriek of pure lust, arched her back, and ground herself into his groin. This triggered the hot flood that had been building behind the dam of his self-control.

Rolling together on the bed, they spent their lust quickly.

"I knew it," Gloria said softly. "From the moment I saw you on the road, I knew you were right for me."

Slocum said nothing as he held her in his arms. Fooling

around with another man's wife, even the wife of a peacock like Lord Benbow, was dangerous. Somehow, he forgot all about his misgivings when Gloria coaxed him into hardness again.

5

For the second time that night, Slocum was awakened by an intruder. The creaking floorboards out in the hallway betrayed the sneak thief. Untangling himself from Gloria Benbow, Slocum pushed off the bed, found his pants, and got into them. Then he drew his six-shooter and went to the door.

He cursed this oversight. After Gloria had come into his room, he had not locked the door. What if Lord Benbow had happened in on them and found his wife in bed with a newly hired "frontier ruffian"? Slocum wasn't as concerned with what the fop might try to do to him as he was with Samuel Benbow taking it out on his wife.

Slocum wasn't going to let anything happen to Gloria. Anything.

Opening the door a crack confirmed his suspicions. A

dark figure skulked down the hallway, trying each door-knob as he came. Slocum tried to get a good look at the man's face but couldn't. The gaslight had been turned low to save fuel, casting deep shadows everywhere.

Slocum started to close the door and let the thief ply his trade when he saw the man stop in front of the Benbows' door. He turned the knob, but it was locked. At this Slocum frowned. If Gloria had locked the door before slipping into his room, where had she put the key? She had been delightfully—and totally—naked and he hadn't seen the key.

But the door to her room was locked. And the sneak thief was working to force the lock.

The sharp snap signaled the lock breaking. Like mist blown by the wind, the thief disappeared into the room across the hall.

Slocum wasted no time following. He stepped barefoot into the hall and avoided any creaking floorboards as he positioned himself before the other door. He cocked his Colt, then opened the door.

The thief searched through Samuel Benbow's trunk, tossing clothing out, obviously searching for something other than lavender-scented underwear.

"Hold it right there," Slocum said in a level voice. "I've got you covered."

The warning fell on deaf ears. The thief feinted right and dived to the left, scuttling under the bed. Slocum fired and missed. Then he heard a second shot and felt white-hot pain in his ankle. The thief had fired at the only target available from under the bed.

Falling forward, Slocum landed on the springy bed. He judged where the thief must be, then fired through the mattress. This report was muffled and the slug barely got through the thickness of comforter, blanket, and mattress. Before Slocum could fire again, he was startled to feel the bed rising under him.

The burglar hoisted the entire bed and pinned Slocum

between the mattress and the rear wall. When the bed came crashing down, Slocum's aim was off. He fired and missed the man as he fled the room.

Scrambling to get his feet under him, Slocum followed warily. The robber had a pistol and had fired one round. He might have five more to use on Slocum.

Hobbling slightly, Slocum knew he would never be able to follow the thief in his present condition. He rushed back to his room.

"John, what's going on? I heard shots and you were gone."

"Thief. In your room," Slocum got out as he tugged on his boots. He grabbed his shirt and said, "Stay here until I get back. Don't open the door for anyone else."

"But John!"

He ran to the end of the hall and saw the open window used by the thief to make his escape. Slocum had no hope of tracking the robber until he saw a smear on the windowsill. He ran his finger along the wood and it came away with sticky, fresh blood.

"Winged him," Slocum said, startled that his shot through the mattress had been the least bit effective. He climbed out the window and dropped hard to the ground. There Slocum began his tracking in earnest. The drops of blood grew larger as he followed the wetness on the ground. The thief was hightailing it in the direction of the livery stable.

Once he realized this, Slocum stopped following the trail and went directly to the hostler's.

A man inside the stables struggled to get his foot into a stirrup. Slocum saw him try and fail three times before knowing the reason. The bullet had caught the man in the upper thigh. From the dark patch on the man's jeans, Slocum knew he must have hit an artery. The man was bleeding to death by inches—and they might not even be slow inches.

"Get your hands up," Slocum called, his Colt cocked and aimed.

"You're not takin' me in!" cried the man. Slocum fired as the man fumbled for the six-shooter tucked into his belt. The shot hit the thief high in the shoulder, spinning him around. For a moment Slocum's target was blocked by the rearing horse. When the horse ran from the stable, Slocum moved closer.

The man's tenacity almost cost Slocum his life. The fallen thief rolled over and raised his six-gun with both hands. He got off a shot that creased Slocum's arm. He might have taken the thief alive then because the gun sagged, but Slocum's reflexes took over.

He fired a death-dealing round squarely into the man's heart. Without another sound, the robber flopped back in the straw.

"What's going on here?" came the aggrieved demand. "If you lift that six-shooter in my direction, you're a dead man."

Slocum glanced over his shoulder and saw a familiar face.

"I caught this man rifling through . . ." Slocum hesitated. Did he want to tell the sheriff he had caught the thief in Lord Benbow's room while Lady Benbow was in another man's bed?

". . . through my employer's room. Scared his wife something fierce," Slocum lied.

"Who might you be?"

"Name's Slocum, Sheriff Plummer."

"I recognize you now. You were getting a shave the other morning when that road agent got gunned down." Henry Plummer squinted hard at Slocum, as if this might force the truth from his lips.

"You've got a good memory for faces," Slocum said. He heard a slight New England accent in Plummer's words. "Do you know him?" Slocum pointed to the dead man.

"I've seen him in town. A no-account drifter, from all reports," Plummer allowed. "Never heard of him rifling through hotel guests' belongings before, though." Plummer went over and kicked the dead man in the ribs a couple times to be sure of his condition. "You're a mighty good shot. Plugged him smack in the heart."

"Missed before," Slocum said.

"Not so it mattered." Plummer studied the blood smearing the dead man's pants leg. "He would have bled to death before he'd gone a mile."

"Then we're even. He's dead and he didn't take anything."

Henry Plummer looked up, startled. Then he laughed. "You've got a sense of humor, Slocum. But it'll take more than that in Bannack to keep you out of the calaboose."

Slocum heard movement behind him. He remembered the two deputies that had trailed Plummer into the barbershop. He didn't have to be told they stood behind him now, their six-shooters drawn and aimed at his back.

"All I've told you is the truth, Sheriff."

"Reckon that will be up to a judge and jury. I've got a dead man who's not going to tell any lies—or any truths, for all that. I don't rightly know you, so we have to let the court settle the matter."

A deputy reached around and pulled the six-gun from Slocum's grip. Another six-shooter was shoved hard into his back.

"Get him on over to the jailhouse, Bill."

"Right away, Sheriff," came a voice that sounded vaguely familiar to Slocum. He studied the deputy's craggy face and wondered where their paths had crossed before. He worried it might have been in some other town. Slocum had enough wanted posters following him through the West for it to be a problem if he encountered a lawman with a good memory.

The deputy didn't show any sign of recognizing Slocum.

This was about the only good news Slocum could see.

"I shot in self-defense," Slocum called as the deputy shoved him toward the stable doors.

"The judge will decide all that," Henry Plummer said in his soft voice. For all the low, even quality in the sheriff's tone, Slocum heard the icy edge to it. Sheriff Plummer was not a man to cross.

"When will the judge ride through on his circuit?" Slocum asked the deputy.

"Can't rightly say. In a week or two. Might be as long as a month. No set schedule. Don't go worrying your head none over it," the deputy said, shoving Slocum through the door into the small jailhouse. "We'll feed you—when we remember to."

The deputy laughed at that. Slocum would have made a break for it then and there if a second deputy hadn't crowded close behind. In the street Slocum saw several more of Plummer's men gathered, the stars on their chests all gleaming in the gaslight from the office. He could never fight this small army.

"I killed a sneak thief in self-defense," Slocum protested. "You ought to be out rounding up the road agents working along the route to Helena and Salt Lake City."

The deputy laughed harshly, his weather-beaten face turning even craggier. "Don't go telling Sheriff Plummer what he ought to do—and what he shouldn't do. He's not one to take kindly to such intrusion."

Again Slocum tried to remember where he had seen the deputy before. His examination caused the deputy to glare at him.

"What's wrong, prisoner? Never see such a handsome face before?" The sneer would have curdled milk.

Slocum said nothing as he let the lawman put him in a cell at the rear of the jailhouse. To Slocum's surprise, the other three cells were empty. Plummer ran Bannack with an iron hand, but apparently didn't jail many. The cemetery outside town probably got more than its fair share of prisoners, Slocum decided.

The clang of the metal door closing sent a shiver down Slocum's spine. He prowled about the cage for a few minutes, hunting for any weakness. If there was one, he missed it. Iron straps held with rivets ran every few inches. He could hardly reach outside the cell, much less squeeze his entire body through. The solitary window was high on the wall and securely covered by both the metal straps making up the cell and iron bars embedded in solid stone.

It would take a few sticks of dynamite to blow open this jail. Even if Slocum had such explosives, he would never use them. There would be nothing but bloody paste left of him if he tried using enough to blast his way out.

Dropping onto the hard straw-filled mattress, he reflected that the bed in the Royal Hotel had been a sight more comfortable. And that bed had Gloria Benbow in it too.

The thought of his employer's wife made Slocum sit up. He worked out a dozen different lies to explain why Gloria was in his room rather than her own, but he doubted he would need any of them when his trial came around. Unless Plummer changed his mind, the judge was likely to call Slocum's shooting of the sneak thief a murder.

Slocum rubbed his neck, wondering how long it might hurt when they hanged him.

He lay back and tried to sleep, but could not. His mind kept skipping from one thing to the next. Plummer. The deputy. What had the thief been hunting? From his single-minded entry and search of the Benbows' room, he had been hunting for something more than a few dollars and Gloria Benbow's jewelry.

His thoughts were disturbed by a commotion in the outer office.

"I say, old man, where is your good High Sheriff?"

"High Sheriff?"

"Why, yes, whatever you call the stalwart responsible

for maintaining the peace in this frontier hell.''

Slocum recognized Samuel Benbow's voice. And Henry Plummer's.

"You want something from me?'' Plummer asked calmly. The door leading to the street closed. Slocum pictured the sheriff following Benbow into the office, where the Englishman had accosted the deputy.

"I understand you have incarcerated a retainer of mine. I demand his immediate release.''

"Retainer? You mean a galoot about six foot tall, green eyes, dark hair?''

Slocum was surprised Plummer had taken in so many details in the dark stable. Underestimating the man would prove fatal.

"Why, yes, that sounds like the bloke. John Slocum is his name. A sneak thief entered our room, frightened my wife out of her wits, then headed for the high country, I think the colloquialism is, when our Mr. Slocum accosted him. I came to see what had transpired.''

"You saying Slocum chased the thief out of your hotel room?''

"Amid some gunfire, yes, he did. My wife and I were in bed when the pilferer tried to rob us in the dead of night.''

"You saw the robber with a gun?'' Plummer sounded incredulous.

"I did not *see* it, not exactly. Rather, I saw the flame from the bore when he fired at Mr. Slocum.''

Slocum's eyes narrowed at this blatant lie. Lord Benbow had told one whopper after another to the sheriff, and with quite a ring of sincerity to it all. Benbow had not been in the room, and certainly not in bed with his wife. There was no way he could have seen the fight as he described—it had never happened.

Plummer and Benbow talked a bit more, and finally the door leading to the cell block opened. The deputy came in reluctantly to open the door to Slocum's cell.

"You're free to go," the deputy said with grudging admiration. "Not many get out of here, 'cept to swing at the end of a rope."

In the office Plummer and Benbow continued their animated conversation. Plummer actually laughed at something Lord Benbow said.

"There you are, Slocum. I do declare, it is so hard finding vassals these days who don't take the first chance to lie down on the job," said Benbow.

"What of the thief?" Slocum asked.

"He's dead, nothing was taken, all's well," said Sheriff Plummer. "Let's call it even."

"All right," Slocum said, getting his Colt Navy back from the deputy. He settled it on his left hip, then made a point of putting the leather keeper over the hammer to show he had no intention of using the six-shooter again that night.

"Lord Benbow's spoken highly of you and your service to him and his wife," Henry Plummer said. "Not often we have such civilized visitors to our gold mining town."

"I really must return to the hotel," Benbow said. "Beauty sleep, you understand." He winked broadly at Plummer, clapped Slocum on the shoulder, and said, "Crack of dawn, old chap. I expect to see it all!" With that Samuel Benbow went off into the night, singing a song about a drunken sailor.

"You picked a strange one to work for, Slocum," Plummer said, watching Benbow vanish down the street.

"He convinced you I was innocent of murder," Slocum pointed out.

"Buy you a drink?" offered Plummer.

"I'd be happy to accept. My gullet is parched right about now," Slocum said, puzzling over the sheriff's offer. Plummer didn't seem the kind to lock up a man for murder one minute, then buy him a drink the next.

Slocum felt the deputy's cold stare on him as he left. He

could worry about the man recognizing him later. At the moment, he wanted to find out more about Sheriff Plummer and his motives.

They sauntered down the street to a small saloon in a pitched tent. There had been a wooden sign out front once, but drunken miners and cowboys had blasted it into splinters, making it unreadable. The name of the saloon hardly mattered to Slocum. He found himself needing a drink bad.

"Set 'em up, Pop," Henry Plummer called to the old bartender. The man hobbled over and put a bottle and two glasses in front of the sheriff. The barkeep didn't bother pouring.

Plummer did the honors, hoisting his glass and saluting Slocum with it. "To law-abiding citizens everywhere," the sheriff toasted.

Slocum downed his drink, and was surprised when Plummer immediately filled the empty shot glass.

"How long you been traveling with the Englishman and his wife?" Plummer asked.

Slocum knew then he was in for a grilling, but on a different subject. He wondered how honest he ought to be with the lawman.

"Quite a spell actually," Slocum said. "Best job I've had in well nigh a year."

"A year, eh?" Plummer nodded, accepting this as the time Slocum had worked for Lord Benbow. "Can be short or damned long. Why, I've been out West for over five years now."

"From New England?" asked Slocum.

"You've got a good ear. My people come from Maine." As he spoke, he walked a silver dollar from finger to finger on one hand. Slocum admired the agility shown. But more than this, he saw the spotless six-shooter in the sheriff's holster had seldom been fired. This puzzled him a mite until the man leaned forward, his coat opening. Stuffed into a vest pocket was a derringer worn slick from hard use.

Slocum put this into his mind. If he ever crossed Henry Plummer, he would watch not the six-gun but the derringer.

As they talked, the sheriff's suave demeanor turned more surly. He had been intelligent, even witty, when sober and Slocum figured the women, such as they were in a mining town like Bannack, would flock to be with the handsome sheriff. But a few shots of liquor in him turned him into a mean drunk.

"Lord Benbow's a hard master," Slocum said after a few more drinks. "Better tend to his rig and get it ready for the morning scout, as he calls it."

"A harsh master," mused Plummer. "But you earn your keep, I'd wager, Slocum. And have for a solid year?"

The way the sheriff left the question hanging told Slocum Plummer was not going to accept his word at face value. For some reason, Plummer was more interested in Lord Benbow than he was in a man who had gunned down a thief.

Or was it Samuel Benbow the sheriff wanted to learn more about? Gloria Benbow was a mighty fine-looking woman. A handsome rogue sporting considerable power like Henry Plummer would consider her fair game—if her husband turned up missing or dead.

"See you around, Sheriff," Slocum said, wishing Plummer would simply vanish from the face of the planet.

The cold Montana night washed away the alcoholic fog that had drifted over Slocum's mind. He walked briskly back to the Royal Hotel, wondering what new problems he would find there.

6

Slocum paused, hand on the faceted glass doorknob of his hotel room. Would Gloria Benbow be waiting for him in his bed? He glanced back at the door leading to Lord Benbow's room. The splintered doorjamb had not been fixed, but Slocum hadn't expected it to be at this time of night. The hotel clerk probably knew nothing of the attempted robbery yet. What lay behind that crudely closed door? The lord and his lady? Or something else?

Twisting hard on the doorknob, Slocum went into his room. For a moment, he stood and started at the bed. Then he let out a sigh of resignation. Among the rumpled sheets he saw only a carelessly tossed pillow and nothing more. Certainly no Lady Benbow.

Slocum shucked off his worn shirt and pulled off his boots. He unbuckled his gun belt and laid it atop the pile of clothes on a nearby chair before lying down in the bed. As tired as he was, sleep refused to come easily. Every breath he took filled his nostrils with Gloria's insidious perfume. And with the fragrant scent came memories.

It didn't make sense, not really. Lord Benbow was not much of a man, or so it seemed to Slocum. He could understand why a hot-blooded woman like Gloria sought another man's bed. But how far her husband would go if he happened to find out was a question Slocum wasn't prepared to answer. He felt he owed the man for lying to the sheriff and getting him out of jail.

Why Benbow had done it was beyond Slocum's ability to guess, but he owed Samuel Benbow for that. Cuckolding the man wasn't any way of repaying the service. Slocum decided it was best for him to hightail it before dawn and to hell with answering all the questions boiling so vigorously around him.

Sheriff Plummer had seemed a mite more interested in Lord Benbow than he ought to. And what had the thief been hunting for in Benbow's room? With these questions rattling around in his skull, Slocum dropped off to a troubled sleep.

He came immediately awake when someone knocked loudly on his door. Slocum sat upright in bed, eyes widening at the sight of light slanting through his window to leave warm streaks on the threadbare carpet. He had intended to be gone by now.

"Slocum, get your gear. I want a first-rate tour of this fine mining boom town today. I am not paying you to sleep away the entire morning."

"Be right there," Slocum called, reaching for his clothing. Outside he heard Benbow greeting his wife. Slocum stopped grabbing wildly for his clothes and dropped to one knee, peering through the keyhole at the couple in the hallway. He frowned.

He expected some show of affection between the two.

There was none. They stood a chaste distance apart, speaking in voices too low for him to overhear. Gloria reached out and touched Samuel Benbow on the arm, finally stood on tiptoe, and lightly kissed his cheek. Then she rushed off down the hall.

This hardly seemed the way a wife would part company from her husband, unless customs were different in England. Slocum shook his head as he finished dressing. He strapped down his gun belt and made sure the Colt Navy slid easily in the holster. He had the feeling he was going to need his six-shooter soon.

"There you are, old chap. Capital. Where do we explore this fine day?"

"Reckon you and Lady Benbow ought to get some breakfast first," Slocum said. "Nothing like a rasher of bacon, some grits, and fried potatoes for breakfast to get you braced for the day's exploration."

"Gloria and I have already eaten," Benbow said, delicately patting his lips. "I say, is it usual for you frontier chaps to sleep so late? It is almost seven o'clock."

"I want to thank you for vouching for me last night," Slocum said, avoiding the implication he was a slugabed. "I'd still be locked up if you hadn't lied to the sheriff."

Slocum watched Lord Benbow carefully. The man never blinked an eye as he said, "Quite all right. The least I could do for a loyal servant, you know."

Slocum started to press him on how he had lied, then realized Benbow played the same game he did—avoiding the truth. Slocum wondered at Benbow's motives.

"Where do we go first?" Benbow asked. "I would look over a mine, if possible. I understand quite a lot of silver and gold is taken from the hills up and down Alder Gulch."

"Gold," Slocum said. "It's not usual to find silver alongside gold mines. This isn't the richest—not equal to the Nevada Comstock Lode—but several million dollars' worth of metal has been pulled from the ground over the past few years.''

''Splendid. We *must* see one of these fine factories of earthly wealth,'' Benbow said, heading down the steps into the hotel lobby and letting Slocum trail after him. ''Bring the carriage around, and we shall get started on this new adventure.''

Slocum watched the Englishman strut down the middle of the street, looking about as if everything were new and wonderful. Slocum wondered how Benbow could miss the horse dung in the streets, the dogs yipping and pissing on every hitching post, the filth that piled up since no one cared to dispose of it.

He made his way off Bannack's main street and followed back ways to the stable, intending to mount his new horse and ride out of town. It wasn't the most honorable thing he had ever done, but sleeping with Benbow's wife hadn't been either. By leaving now, Slocum avoided further unpleasantness.

If sleeping with a beautiful woman could ever be considered unpleasant, especially one as knowing and eager as Gloria Benbow.

''You're leaving us, aren't you?''

Slocum swung about guiltily. He faced the very woman he had been thinking about so hard.

''We shouldn't have passed the night together, Lady Benbow,'' he said. ''It wasn't right.''

''Are you having an attack of morals? My, I misjudged you, John. And don't call me Lady Benbow. My name is Gloria.'' She moved closer, her perfume making his nostrils flare in memory of the passion they had shared the night before. The dark-haired beauty ran her fingers up and down the front of his shirt. Slocum felt himself melting inside—and hardening elsewhere.

''I'm no Southern gentleman,'' Slocum said, ''but I

know what's right and what's not. Sleeping with another man's wife is wrong.''

"Even if she wanted it so desperately?" Gloria moved closer. Her breasts brushed against him now. He felt the heat from her body.

"It wasn't proper," he said doggedly. "You've got a reputation to protect."

"Repu—?" Gloria looked startled for a moment, then laughed in delight. "That's rich, John. You're worried about my reputation!"

"I'm not sure what's going on in Bannack, but my leaving will keep the peace a spell longer," Slocum said. "The sheriff was mighty interested in your husband last night."

"After Samuel got you out of jail?" Gloria smiled crookedly, as if enjoying a private joke.

"He lied to the sheriff. He said the two of you were in your room when the sneak thief came in. Why would Lord Benbow say something that wasn't true?"

"Don't fret over it. Samuel is nothing if not pragmatic. He sees your value to us—as a guide. He has never enjoyed good relations with the law."

"In England?"

Gloria's face snapped upward to study Slocum's. Her blue eyes turned into limitlessly deep pools. Slocum tried to fathom them and what went on behind, in her mind. He failed.

"I knew from the moment we came across one another you weren't a simple cowboy. You might take a bit of advice, John. Don't think too much. It could get you in real trouble."

It was Slocum's turn to laugh harshly. Since arriving in Montana he had seen nothing but trouble. His horse breaking a leg, the winter living on little more than roots and diseased rabbits, the abortive gold robbery and the chase by the road agents, his night with Gloria and in jail. Trouble came at him from all directions.

Some of it was just more enjoyable getting into.

"You want me to show you around Bannack?" Slocum asked.

"As a personal favor, John. Please. Don't vanish on me." Gloria's tone changed to one of pleading. Slocum was never sure if he confronted a masterful actress in Lady Benbow or simply saw emotions she worked to hide from others. "Please?"

"I've never been a guide like this," he admitted. "It's hard to know what you might enjoy seeing."

"Oh, things," she said ambiguously.

"I can do that." Slocum tapped the wad of greenbacks still riding in his pocket. Somehow, neither Sheriff Plummer nor his deputy had taken the roll from him. It was just as well. If they had pulled the bills from his pocket, they might have noticed the grains of gold dust there.

Explaining that away would have taken more guile than Lord Benbow had displayed.

"Your husband wanted me to fetch the carriage, but I have a better idea. There are things to do around town that might give you a few good stories to tell back in England."

"You intrigue me," Gloria said. "And so does your mysterious proposal."

She laughed at his distraction, then took his arm, and together they left the stables. It took only a few minutes to find Lord Benbow hunkering down on the boardwalk near an old-timer, trying to squeeze precious stories of the old days from him.

"You won't have much luck on that score, Lord Benbow," Slocum said. "Bannack's a boom town. It didn't exist ten years ago." He looked at the old codger and got a broken-toothed grin from him. Slocum tipped his hat and went on.

"I have an idea that might appeal to you both," Slocum said, pointing toward one of three general stores along the main street. "Why not get outfitted for a proper ride in the country? That is as good a place as any to get authentic Western gear.''

''I knew I could trust you to come up with delightful things for us, Slocum. Come along, my dear. Why didn't we think of this?''

Slocum followed them into the store and spent a few minutes discussing with the proprietor how far he could fleece his English customers. The store owner rubbed his hands together and went to work selling gear that had gathered dust in his store for a year or more.

Slocum left the two to their shopping and went outside. His belly rumbled, but he didn't have time for a proper breakfast. He fished about in the pickle barrel and got a thick one, then settled down in a chair to wait for the Benbows to finish inside.

He had taken only a few bites of the pickle when he saw Henry Plummer and a miner in the alley beside the store. Slocum rocked back in his chair and cocked his head to one side to better eavesdrop on what the sheriff was telling the grizzled old prospector.

He almost fell from his chair when he heard Sheriff Plummer say, ''The roads in these parts are safer than anywhere else in Montana Territory. You can bet your life on that.''

''Well, Sheriff, I heard different.'' The old miner sounded skeptical.

''Don't go listening to my opponents. I beat too many in fair elections for them to say good things about me. You've seen how I run Bannack.''

''Nice town, clean enough and no trouble.''

''Never any trouble,'' Plummer lied with a straight face. ''I have a pack of deputies to prevent any trouble. I keep everyone in line, both here and all up and down Alder Gulch.''

''That's good to hear. I reckon I can tell you, I'm mighty skittish about traveling with so much gold. I been up in the hills for almost a year on my claim.''

"It's good to keep such a large amount secret," Plummer said. "I'd offer to send a deputy along with you, but that might attract unwanted attention.''

"If there's no road agents workin' the Gulch road, what's it matter?'' the miner demanded.

"I have better uses for my deputies here in Bannack," Plummer countered. "I can't remember the last time anyone got robbed in my county,'' the sheriff declared.

"Maybe I ought to have got into town more, so's I'd know.''

"Why would I lie to you? You'll be as safe as if you were in your mama's arms again,'' Plummer stated firmly. "You'll be in Helena before you know it, safe and filling the bank vault there with your metal.''

"But there *is* a chance there might be robbers on the road you don't know about,'' the miner said, obviously unwilling to accept Plummer's word that the sheriff had flushed out all the criminals from the county.

"Come along,'' Plummer said, putting his arm around the miner's shoulders and pulling him close. "I'll tell you how to avoid the main road. Might even be a tad quicker getting to Helena, but the going is more difficult. Rocky road,'' Plummer said.

Slocum tried to remember other roads leading from Alder Gulch to Helena and couldn't.

"That's mighty generous of you, Sheriff.''

"You won't be sorry you came to me for advice,'' Plummer assured the miner. "Now listen close. This is a secret road, and I don't want you spreading it around. Only the truly large gold shipments go this route, and I don't want it known.''

The route Plummer detailed for the miner took the man—and his gold—smack into the middle of the outlaw country by the large red monolithic rock.

"You get on the road now,'' Plummer urged. As the

miner passed by where Slocum sat chewing on the last of his pickle, Slocum saw the sheriff take a large piece of chalk from his coat pocket and draw a hooklike symbol on the canvas covering the load on the miner's mule.

Henry Plummer strode off, whistling to himself. He had not seen Slocum spying on his conversation with the miner. Slocum started to call the miner back, then decided on a different way of answering some of the questions that were popping up around him.

"How do we look, John?" Gloria Benbow came from the general store and did a quick pirouette so he could see every curve of her body encased in tight-fitting jeans and a man's shirt that strained to hold in her ample breasts. She wore a blue bandanna at her swanlike throat and had tucked the tops of her jeans into gaudy boots.

"Never seen a prettier sight," Slocum said truthfully. He had to force himself to keep from laughing when he saw Lord Benbow decked out in a similar costume. On him it looked ridiculous.

"I certainly feel more like a cowboy now," Samuel Benbow declared, swinging a tall black hat about and slapping it against his thigh. All Slocum could do was silently thank the store owner that he had not also sold Benbow a six-gun to strap on. Not only would Lord Benbow have looked like a greenhorn then, he would have drawn gunfighters like flies to decaying meat. Somewhere along the way, Benbow would have been forced to use any sidearm.

"Let's go for a ride," Slocum said. "I'll bring the carriage around." He hurried to the stable, got the horse hitched, and then tied his own horse's reins to the back of the carriage. He jumped in and got the rig around to the general store before too many of Bannack's citizens saw the comical sight of the Englishman and his wife in their store-bought duds.

"Where do we head, Slocum?" asked Benbow.

"I heard of a road off the main course that leads back

into the hills. We might find a prospector or two willing to show you their claims,'' Slocum said, intending on following the old miner the sheriff had misdirected. He was curious about not only the directions the miner had been given, but about the curious marking Plummer had put on the canvas as the mule passed him.

They rode along, Slocum intent on finding the miner. He worried Benbow might want a running commentary about the terrain, but the Englishman kept himself amused with odd observations about the countryside and its vegetation. Gloria found her husband's comments amusing. Slocum was content to let the two chatter away like magpies. It wasn't difficult, but he wanted to be sure he didn't lose the trail.

A mile outside Bannack a dusty track cut into the hills. Slocum tried to imagine how this route could ever reach Helena, and couldn't. In that general direction lay what he had started thinking of as Road Agent Rock, the huge monolith of bright red where he had stirred up a hornet's nest of outlaws.

''There seems little enough mining up here, Slocum,'' observed Benbow. ''Are you sure this is an appropriate—''

''There, up ahead,'' Slocum said. He spotted the old prospector making his way along, leading his heavily laden mule. And in the rocks above the miner lay a half-dozen armed men.

''I say, they are going to waylay that aged gentleman!''

The words were hardly out of Lord Benbow's mouth when the road agents opened fire on the miner.

7

Slocum jumped down from the carriage and ran to his horse. He pulled out his rifle and cocked the Winchester even as he was turning. The rifle butt came to his shoulder, and he fired in the same instant. The shot went wide of its mark, but the road agent jumped, lost his balance, and fell off the boulder.

"You hit him!" cried Gloria, clapping her hands.

"Missed," Slocum said glumly. He snapped to the two in the carriage as he raced by them, "Stay here and keep down." A dozen paces closer to the miner, Slocum fired again. This time he winged one of the outlaws intent on bushwhacking the miner. But they had turned their rifles in his direction now, realizing the miner posed no danger for them—and Slocum did.

Slocum had anticipated that; he wanted to be as far from

the Benbows as possible when the owlhoots opened fire on him. He fell facedown in the dust and got off two more quick shots. Neither hit an outlaw, but they did drive them back under cover.

"That's the way, son!" crowed the old miner. "Give 'em hell!"

"Keep down," Slocum ordered the excited hardrock miner. He wiggled forward, then stopped and put his ear to the rocky ground. He heard the thunder of hooves. He had driven off the robbers. Pushing to his feet, he dusted himself off.

"You done run them varmints off. Thank you kindly," the miner said. "They was gonna rob me for sure."

"I'm afraid so," Slocum said. He went to the side of the mule and ran his finger over the curving white chalk sign put on the canvas by Sheriff Plummer.

"What's that?"

"One of the road agents marked you for robbery," Slocum said grimly. He had never trusted Henry Plummer, but now he knew enough to implicate the lawman. But who would believe him? It would be his word against that of a respected—and feared—sheriff.

"Don't know how that sheriff of yours coulda put me on such a dangerous path," the miner said, scratching himself and shaking his head. "It's right crazy. Musta taken the wrong road."

"Capital, simply superb. I never imagined we would be privileged to witness a gunfight!" Samuel Benbow strode forward, thumbs tucked into his belt and trying to swagger. Gloria followed a few paces behind.

"What are you, son? Part of a side show?"

"No, old-timer," Slocum said, not wanting to explain. "If you're still in one piece, why not get back on the main road and make for Helena as fast as this mule will go? I don't think you will have any more trouble."

"Why's that?"

Slocum didn't bother explaining his idea that, once the road agents were sent out, others in their gang would not try to duplicate effort. Running his finger over the curious marking on the canvas convinced him to leave it there. The road agents along the main road would see it and think others in their band had been dispatched to rob the miner. One problem with a military organization was strict adherence to orders.

"Just get on along, and be careful. I might be wrong about there not being any more highwaymen out today."

"All right. You take care now, son, and don't let them two funny-dressed folks tell you what to do." The grizzled miner scratched himself again and tugged to get his mule headed back to the main road.

"I say, old chap," called Samuel Benbow to the miner, "how large a cargo of gold are you carrying?"

The miner ignored the question and shouted at Slocum, "They'll get you killed if you don't keep 'em quiet, them and their funny duds." With a shake of his head, the miner hastened back along the rude path Henry Plummer had set him on.

"An ingrate," Lord Benbow said, making a sour face. "What do you plan to do now, Slocum?"

"Samuel, please, we ought to return to Bannack and—"

"You two can get back to town by yourselves," Slocum said. "I am going to track down the road agents." He untied his horse from the carriage and tried to remember the lay of the land. Too many confusing canyons lay between him and Road Agent Rock, where he expected to find the outlaws' main encampment. Slocum wasn't sure what he would do when he found their main bivouac, but the federal marshals up in Helena might be willing to pay a small reward for the location.

"We shall do no such thing!" exclaimed Benbow. "We will accompany you."

"Only if you can keep up," Slocum said, unwilling to argue. He figured he could lose them in a mile or less. They could get back to Bannack before sundown, even if they walked.

"Very well," Benbow said. He and Gloria unhitched the horse from the carriage. Slocum watched as the pair mounted it bareback. They had some equestrian skills, he decided. They rode more easily than he would have thought.

Slocum ranged out, leading his horse in a wide arc until he found freshly spilled blood. He dropped to one knee and tried to figure out which direction the wounded road agent had gone.

"That way," Samuel Benbow said, pointing into a tumble of rocks. "He went that way."

Slocum started to make a rude comment, then saw fresh spoor leading in the direction Benbow was pointing. He frowned, wondering if the Englishman had gotten lucky or if there was more to him than met the eye. Benbow rode expertly and had picked up the faint trail before Slocum.

"The going gets rough now," Slocum said. "Those robbers won't take kindly to anyone following them."

"You go along. We'll not hold you back, John," Gloria said.

He shot her a cold look. She had used his first name, but her husband had not noticed the indiscretion.

Shaking off his annoyance, Slocum set off along the track, leading his horse and finding occasional broken twigs and scuffled dirt to mark the trail. When he reached the far side of a pile of rocks, he found a narrow dirt path and evidence horses had been tethered there. Slocum then mounted and rode along, keeping a sharp eye out for both ambush and any turn his quarry might make off the narrow path.

He remembered the tangle of canyons and trails too well. But Slocum again showed he wasn't sharp enough. From ten yards back, Gloria called out to him.

"John, wait. Come see what Samuel found."

Slocum wheeled his horse about and returned. Lord Benbow was down on his hands and knees, peering along the ground as if he knew what he was doing.

"They went this direction, Slocum," Benbow said. "Two of them, maybe three."

"I didn't see it." Slocum dropped to the ground and sucked in his breath when he saw what Benbow already had. The Englishman had proven himself a better tracker than Slocum. Again.

"From the way the bushes are changing color, there might be a spring up this canyon," Benbow said.

"You're mighty sharp on tracking. Where'd you learn all these tricks?"

Samuel Benbow laughed in delight. "I always enjoyed riding to the hounds. This is a hunt not too dissimilar."

Slocum had heard how the British nobles used packs of hounds to run down a fox. He didn't understand what sport there was in that, any more than he had ever figured what appealed to men about bearbaiting. But from all he knew of the English, they let the dogs find the fox. They didn't sully their fancy riding duds by getting down and studying the ground as Benbow did.

Walking his horse down the faint trail, Slocum quickly discovered Benbow was right about the pond. From deep artesian wells bubbled clear spring water that pooled at the end of the canyon. Slocum let his horse drink as he carefully searched the area. He found one of the impossibly narrow crevices leading away.

"They went down there," Slocum said.

"Only one. The other two—the uninjured ones—went down that way," Benbow said, contradicting him.

Slocum started thinking his skill as a tracker was long gone. Benbow's razor-sharp eyes had again picked out the truth among all the muddled clues left by the road agents.

"I'm going after the injured outlaw," Slocum decided. "He might be a tad easier to stop." He didn't bother mentioning he thought the owlhoot might also be heading back to the main camp to lick his wounds. Catching crooks wasn't what Slocum wanted as much as finding a trail to the huge red monolith.

Road Agent Rock.

"Tally-ho," cried Benbow, smiling. Slocum glanced at Gloria, who said nothing. He tried to read her expression and failed.

Slocum led his horse into the crevice, followed by the Benbows, and immediately picked up the pace, wanting to run. The narrow, sheer walls of rock threatened to crush in on him. When he looked up, it seemed the rims were bending over, ready to drop rocks on his head. Tight places seldom bothered Slocum. This did.

He heaved a sigh of relief when the crevice opened into a familiar valley. Slocum was certain he had ranged up and down this grassy expanse before.

"There he is," Slocum said, climbing into the saddle. "Not a mile ahead of us. You stay back, out of range. There might be some shooting."

Slocum didn't wait for Benbow and Gloria to emerge from the fissure. He put his heels to the horse's flanks and galloped off in pursuit of the road agent. He got within a hundred yards before the wounded man realized he was in any danger.

When the outlaw saw Slocum pounding down the sloping valley, he tried to urge his tired horse to run. But he was too late to ever get away. Slocum overtook him within a few hundred yards.

"Stop!" Slocum yelled, but the outlaw wasn't going to surrender easily. He bent forward and tried to get more speed from his flagging horse.

Slocum rode closer, then kicked free of his stirrups and

grabbed for the outlaw. Hand closing on the wounded man's shirt, Slocum yanked and let his weight do the rest of the work for him. Outlaw and Slocum tumbled to the ground, hitting hard and rolling. Slocum was dazed from the fall, and the outlaw beat him back to his feet.

"You're gonna die, you son of a bitch," the outlaw cried. He grabbed at the six-gun stuck in his belt, but his wounded shoulder turned him clumsy. He fumbled at the butt of his six-shooter and let Slocum roll over, get his feet under him, and dive parallel to the ground.

Slocum's shoulder hit the outlaw smack in the belly. They went down again, this time with Slocum coming out on top. Grabbing, Slocum got the road agent's pistol away from him and tossed it aside.

"You're coming with me all the way to Helena. The federal marshal will want to hear about all the robberies you've committed—and I want to know where your camp is."

Thought of piles of gold raced across Slocum's mind. If he got there before the law, he might help himself to a bit of that gold. These highwaymen had done him out of a strongbox load of gold dust already. It was only fitting they donate a little of their ill-gotten gains to make up for his inconvenience.

Slocum wasn't sure what warned him first. The change in the captive outlaw's expression. Some sound he barely heard. The movement of a shadow across the ground. Slocum went for his Colt at the same time he rolled away from his captive.

As he spun about, he fought to get his Colt Navy from its holster. He had left the leather thong over the hammer so it wouldn't fall out while he was riding. Now his oversight in leaving the keeper on was going to mean his death.

He stared down the huge bore of a Sharps buffalo gun aimed directly at his face.

The outlaw holding the heavy rifle smiled, a gold tooth gleaming in the bright Montana sunlight.

"See you in Hell," the outlaw said.

Slocum could do nothing but die.

8

Slocum closed his eyes as an ear-splitting shot rang out. For a moment, Slocum wondered why searing pain hadn't visited him, followed by a slow decline into the oblivion of death. His eyes sprang open when he realized the muffled report he heard had not been from a powerful rifle but from a handgun.

The outlaw who had sneaked up on him lay flat on his back on the ground, sightless eyes staring at the blue Montana sky. Samuel Benbow stood to one side, a smoking, small-caliber pistol held confidently in his hand. Behind him, still mounted, Gloria sat comfortably gripping a two-barreled derringer. If her husband had missed the outlaw, she would not have.

Slocum didn't doubt the lovely dark-haired woman could turn into a merciless avenging angel in a flash. She seemed as competent with the small pistol as Benbow did with his larger one.

"Fixed his hash, as you Yanks say," Benbow declared, nudging the dead man with the toe of his gaudy boot.

"Never thought of myself as a Yankee," Slocum said, pushing to his feet. Relief at being alive flooded him. He didn't even mind being called a Yank.

"What are you going to do with that one?" Benbow aimed his five-shot Smith & Wesson rimfire at the road agent Slocum had knocked from horseback. The man struggled weakly, trying to wiggle away like the sidewinder he was, but not getting too far.

"What do you suggest?" Slocum asked. He slipped the keeper off his Colt Navy and felt worlds better for this simple action.

"I could shoot him," Benbow said in an offhand manner. "I've never killed two men in one day. That would be quite a hoot, wouldn't you say, my darling?"

"You need something special to tell the Explorers Club when you return to England," Gloria said, a small smile dancing on her lips.

"You don't scare me none!" shouted the fallen outlaw. "I seen hundreds of men kilt in a day and it didn't bother me none."

The outlaw turned white when Benbow fired and shot off the top of his left ear.

"My, he moved. I intended to put the round between his eyes. Maybe the next time," Benbow said, with mock annoyance. He spun the cylinder in his pistol, grinning wickedly.

"It is amazing how an attitude can change so quickly, isn't it?" Gloria observed.

"Quit playing with the owlhoot," Slocum said. He faced the supine outlaw, dark anger bubbling to the surface. The man cringed away from Slocum's wrath.

"I've been shot at, robbed, taken advantage of, put in

jail, and all for nothing," Slocum said. He kept his anger in check and his words level and cold. This frightened the outlaw more than blinding rage would have. "I want information about the road agents and how they operate."

"Oh, I say, ask him a hard question," declared Lord Benbow. "From the man's look, he is not too high up in the road agents' hierarchy. Are you?"

"No, no, I don't know nothing."

"Except who your leader is," said Gloria. "Tell us his name. Please." Her polite request was wreathed in cold-blooded determination. The way she fingered her small gun turned the outlaw even whiter until Slocum thought the man would pass out from fear.

"I'm a private. I don't know things like that. The boss always wears a black hood when he comes around camp. I take my orders from Buck."

"Does Buck have a last name?" asked Slocum.

"You're gonna kill me," the road agent whimpered.

"No," Slocum said, cutting off both Samuel Benbow and his wife. "I don't murder men just because they don't tell me what I want to know. I spent a year or more with the Apaches down in Sonora. You heard of Chief Juh?"

The outlaw shook his head.

"That figures. Most white men he gets his hands on don't live to tell about it. I learned some fine ways of making a man talk," Slocum went on. "Would you like to be tied head down from a tree limb—then have a fire lit under you? A man can last for hours that way, if I don't put too much wood on the fire at first."

"Oh, what a capital idea. All I considered doing was skinning him alive with his own knife," said Benbow, obviously enjoying the byplay.

"That's over too quick. A galoot like this one doesn't have enough skin to last till sundown," Slocum said. "I learned other tortures from the Apaches. Staring into the hot sun with your eyelids cut off makes a man blind within a few seconds, but the pain lasts. Until you die.''

"Look, I don't know much," the man began babbling. "I'm a courier, nothing more."

"They use certain of their number to carry messages," said Benbow. "I hoped we had snared ourselves a sergeant or even a lieutenant in their service. What is your password?"

"Green mountains," the man blurted. "That gets me into all the meetings with the others."

"And the secret sign?"

"A hook. You seen it on the prospector's pack. A hook, like this." The outlaw traced the peculiar symbol in the air for Slocum to study. "I'm not lyin'!"

"I think there is more," said Benbow. "Don't you agree, Slocum?"

"The secret handshake. What is it?"

"I don't know!" the man wailed. "If I get to the next circle of power in the company, then they'll tell me that. I'm just a green recruit."

Slocum dropped to one knee and patted the man's clothing. He felt a thick packet in his right coat pocket. Slocum slipped it out, only to find himself knocked backward as the outlaw got his feet under him and heaved. For an instant, Slocum was between the Benbows and the road agent, preventing them from shooting the fleeing man.

Then a shot rang out. It had the sound of a long-distance report to it, the echo finally catching up with the bullet that had knocked the outlaw to the ground.

Slocum went to the fallen highwayman and rolled him over. The bullet had caught the man in the neck. Slocum knew it had to be a lucky shot—the neck was too small and moving a target for any marksman to hit intentionally. But luck or not, the courier lay dead on the ground.

"We have company," observed Gloria from her perch atop their horse.

Slocum looked down the valley and saw a trio of riders approaching. He stepped away from the dead outlaw and squinted. He caught the glint of sunlight off badges.

"Sheriff Plummer," said Lord Benbow. "What a singular pleasure this is." The Englishman's pistol had vanished back into his clothing. Once more Benbow appeared to be an unarmed fop. Slocum noted that Gloria's derringer had also vanished into her clothing, possibly her boot top from the way her hand lingered on the hand-tooled sides.

"Thought you'd need help. Saw this cayuse and figured he was bad news." Henry Plummer stared down at the dead outlaw. He motioned and his two deputies jumped to the ground. The one named Bill sheathed his rifle. Slocum had misjudged the man's skill. To do so again might spell disaster.

"Come on and give me a hand, Buck," Bill said.

"Aw, Hunter, do I have to?" Buck glanced at Henry Plummer, then at the other deputy. He moved forward hesitantly, as if worrying about ending up dead himself.

Slocum pulled himself straighter. Things began falling into place. He had seen Plummer mark the miner's pack and send him along a route destined to get him robbed. And the two road agents he had identified by name, if not sight, who had chased him before were Hunter and Buck.

Bill Hunter and his partner, Buck. Both deputies. Both working for Henry Plummer.

Slocum figured he knew who the power behind the road agents was.

How he was going to prove it was something else.

"Yep, he's dead, Sheriff," said Hunter.

Slocum watched Buck more carefully. The man turned a little green around the gills. A deputy would have seen dead men. It had to be something more. Maybe Buck didn't cotton much to his partner shooting down a friend as if he were nothing more than a mad dog. Worse, Henry Plummer had probably ordered the killing to keep the man from spilling his guts. Buck might be realizing for the first time what a deadly snake the man he called boss really was.

"We'll take care of this, Slocum. You and the two . . . Brits get on back to Bannack. I'll want to talk to you more about this when we get there."

"All right, Sheriff," Slocum said, knowing better than to argue. He motioned to the Benbows to mount and wheel around.

"You folks know the way back to town?" asked Hunter, eyeing them suspiciously.

"You came from that direction," said Samuel Benbow. "If we follow your tracks, why, I suppose we will come upon Bannack in no time at all!"

The three lawmen watched Slocum and the Benbows leave. The hair on the back of Slocum's neck stood on end as he waited for Bill Hunter's accurate rifle to center on his spine.

For some reason, it never happened. The trio found the main road into town within the hour, and were inside the city limits within two.

Somehow, Slocum felt that returning to Bannack was about the same as turning himself in to the state penitentiary, with no hope of parole.

9

John Slocum felt as if he rode back into a prison cell. He considered taking the road away from Bannack, although the Benbows were eager to find their carriage and ride back into town in the fine style in which they had left. The Englishman thought of himself as a conquering hero, now that adventure had been found in the West.

Every second along the way to Bannack Slocum felt eyes watching him. And those eyes peered down the length of a rifle barrel, putting his head squarely in the sights. The feeling increased when he got to the city limits. Here and there he saw pairs of deputies, standing, watching silently, waiting.

He had no doubt now that Henry Plummer headed the road agents working Alder Gulch. And if Sheriff Plummer were somehow an innocent dupe, his deputy Bill Hunter was not. He had been the outlaw offering a hundred dollars for Slocum's head. The only thing that had saved Slocum was being with Lord Benbow and his wife—that and Hunter possibly not knowing Slocum's identity. From the way the deputy eyed him like a hungry wolf staring at a lamb, Slocum knew Hunter suspected.

Plummer might not be sure of Slocum's intentions, just as Slocum was unable to prove Plummer was the mysterious boss who had organized the gang camping near Road Agent Rock. That standoff also kept Slocum alive. For a while longer.

Slocum whistled tunelessly as he thought. He need not prove anything. He wasn't a lawman—far from it. Getting into this mess had been as simple as having the highwaymen snatch a gold shipment out from under his nose. What struck Slocum as more important was simply getting out of Bannack with his hide in one piece. The instant Plummer—or Hunter—decided he had been the one they had chased throughout their rocky domain, Slocum knew he would be pushing up daisies in the cemetery.

"Why don't you grace us with a ditty, Slocum?"

"What?" Slocum pulled his attention from the deputies watching like buzzards waiting for something to die to Lord Benbow. "How's that?"

"Surely you know some picturesque American tune. 'Little Brown Jug' is a favorite of mine. Or 'Lorena,' I think the name is."

Slocum snorted. That song brought back memories of the war he would as soon forget. He had hired on to guide the Benbows around Bannack, not entertain them.

"My singing is pretty poor. The times I've worked night herd, the beeves all stuffed grass in their ears so they wouldn't have to listen to me."

"How quaint. You really *do* sing to the cows?" asked Gloria.

"Keeps them quiet and the rider awake," Slocum allowed. "You must be tuckered out from all the excitement this morning." He craned his head and tried to get an accurate reckoning of time. He finally pulled out his brother Robert's watch and flipped open the case. It was past three. The lead-gray clouds obscuring the sun promised a heavy rain before sundown.

"We did have more than our share of fun today," said Samuel Benbow.

Slocum looked at him sharply. Something in the man's words didn't jibe with his usual scatterbrained enjoyment of anything having to do with the frontier. Remembering the Smith & Wesson he had tucked away caused Slocum to make a parting comment as Benbow and his wife climbed from the carriage in front of the Royal Hotel.

"In the heat of the moment, I forgot to thank you for saving me back there. You're mighty handy with that hogleg."

"This?" Benbow patted a pocket. "It was nothing. I enjoy setting up clay targets back home and taking potshots at them. It was nothing more than a simple shot, you know."

Slocum shrugged, but he knew better. Benbow had been too cool. There was a world of difference between blasting a clay pigeon into pieces and killing a man. Even if Benbow had not realized the import of what he had done then, during the ride back to Bannack the Englishman ought to have gone into shock at the notion of snuffing out a man's life.

If anything, Benbow appeared more confident than ever and even happy at the day's outcome.

Slocum might have pushed this aside if Gloria Benbow had not been equally untroubled over the sudden death of two men. The derringer in her capable grip had told Slocum she was as likely to have fired as her husband. These two carried more secrets than Slocum had thought when he had agreed to be their guide.

"Get the horses bedded down for the night," Benbow ordered. "And see to the carriage. It has some paint missing here and there. Then come back and we can all find a spot of dinner. I shall treat. You deserve some reward for taking us on this fine quest."

Slocum nodded, but his eyes were locked with Gloria's deep blue ones. He tried to read some emotion there, and failed. The pair was more than he had bargained for.

And the deputies watching his every step to the livery kept him from simply riding from Bannack and never looking back, even if he could have abandoned the Benbows in such a fashion. He had taken Lord Benbow's money and felt obligated to earn it. The thick wad of greenbacks still rode high in his pocket. It might not be as much as he would have gained from the gold robbery, but there was no questioning it amounted to a small fortune.

After tending the animals and arguing with the hostler over fixing the carriage for a fair price, Slocum turned back to the hotel. His earlier suspicions came true. Heavy, large drops of water began tumbling from the sky. By the time he reached the hotel veranda, Bannack's streets had turned into rivers of mud and a stench rose from newly wet garbage piled everywhere.

"Slocum, there you are. Quite a frog strangler, isn't it?" asked Benbow, peering out the hotel window.

"It is," Slocum agreed. Ever since Benbow had drawn the Smith & Wesson and used it with such authority, Slocum had noticed small things about the Englishman he had never bothered with before. Somehow, he could not imagine a proper Englishman ever using the term "frog strangler" with such ease.

"I've decided to dine in the hotel," Benbow declared.

"Where's Mrs. Benbow?"

"Gloria has taken a chill and remains in bed. You are welcome to join me. I did promise you some victuals after today's dustup."

"Thank you kindly," Slocum said, "but I think I might turn in also."

"I intend to go do some serious drinking afterward," Benbow warned. "You might like to accompany me then too."

Slocum shook his head. Benbow laughed and strode off across the lobby, humming "Goober Peas" to himself as he went. Slocum tried to make sense of the English nobleman, and couldn't. Climbing the stairs wearily, Slocum went to his room. He closed the door and dropped onto the bed, suddenly bone tired. Slocum had begged off, not wanting to stay with Benbow this evening, but only now did he realize how tuckered out he really was.

His eyes were turning to lead when he heard the floorboards in the hall creaking, as they had done when the sneak thief had walked along. Slocum came immediately awake, his hand flashing to the ebony butt of his Colt Navy. He paused, then drew and cocked the six-shooter when his door slowly opened.

"John!" cried Gloria Benbow. "Put that away. It's only me."

"You and your derringer?" he asked. Slocum lowered his six-gun but did not holster it.

"You have such a droll sense of humor," she said, sitting on the edge of the bed. The dark-haired woman reached out, her hand resting on his leg. Slocum found himself growing uneasy at the familiar way she touched him. He pulled away.

"John, what's wrong? Don't you find me attractive anymore?" Gloria was toying with him. As she turned, the top buttons of her blouse came free. He caught sight of the creamy swell of her ample breasts. It was everything he could do to force his eyes up and onto her face.

"Have you ever gotten bogged down in quicksand?" he asked.

"Can't say I have," she replied slowly. "What has this to do with me? With us?"

"Not much, perhaps. In case you missed it, we killed two outlaws who have been preying on every stagecoach and freight wagon loaded with gold leaving Bannack. For all I know, those road agents work the entire eighty-mile length of Alder Gulch."

"You're afraid of the robbers?" This seemed to amuse her. She chuckled and, as she shifted about on the bed again, a couple more buttons came unfastened. Slocum saw she wore no undergarments. Her breasts gleamed nakedly in the faint light filtering in the hotel window. When a bolt of lightning crashed nearby and lit the entire sky, he saw those marvelous bosoms in silhouette.

They were perfectly shaped and capped with hard little nipples. Hard. The thought rattled around in his head. They were hard because Gloria wanted him. She had come into his room to make love again.

"The outlaws," he admitted, "are part of it. Making love to another man's wife is a sure way of ending up with a bullet in the back."

"Samuel would never shoot you in the back," Gloria said, startled. "He admires you far too much for that."

"I saw how good he is with that pistol of his. He might not have to shoot me in the back. If he's half as fast as he is a good shot, he might be able to beat me in a fair fight." Slocum doubted this, but wanted to see Gloria's reaction. It was everything he could have wanted.

A banner of emotions fluttered across her face. Another flash of lightning caught her surprise, her amusement, her outright disbelief Slocum could say such a thing. The thunder drowned out part of her reply.

". . . both after the same end," was all he heard.

"What might that be?" Slocum had to ask. "All I want is to get out of Bannack before the road agents gun me down. Right now, they aren't sure how much I know—or can prove. The instant they are certain, I'm a dead man.''

"You know who their leader is, don't you?'' Gloria's blue eyes bored into him.

"Sheriff Plummer leads a right full life,'' Slocum said, dancing around naming the lawman outright. "His deputy, Bill Hunter, and the other one—''

"Buck Stinson,'' Gloria supplied. "And don't forget Forbes and Cleveland and all the other deputies.''

"You know more of them than I do,'' Slocum said, not surprised at Gloria's intimate knowledge. "They all ride with the road agents. Hunter offered a hundred-dollar reward for me, even if he didn't know who he was putting the bounty out on.''

"So it *was* you who tried to hold up the freight wagon the other day!'' Gloria exclaimed. "Samuel heard the rumblings among the road agents about that. They were outraged anyone would try to steal their thunder.'' As if on cue, a new peal of thunder crashed along the streets of Bannack. Gloria scooted closer on the bed.

"Are you going to turn me in for attempted robbery?'' Slocum asked.

"Turn you in? Not if you're real nice to me. *Real* nice.'' Gloria reached over and unbuckled his gun belt. She didn't stop there. Her nimble fingers worked on the buttons holding his jeans.

Slocum wanted to stop her, but he kept seeing flashes of the silken flesh of her breasts, the firm chin, and the set to her features. Gloria was a woman determined to have a man, and Slocum's resolve faded second by second. She was about the most beautiful woman he had ever seen, married or not.

"Your husband said you were in bed with a chill.''

"There's nothing cold about you, John,'' she said, fumbling in his jeans to prove it. "This is what I need.''

"Something hot slipped into you?'' asked Slocum.

Gloria laughed in delight. She shrugged her shoulders

twice and was bare to the waist. The occasional lightning outside limned her like some woodcut print in a fancy book. Slocum reached out and put his hand against her warm cheek.

She turned her face and kissed his palm. Somehow he found himself out of his pants and naked on the bed. Gloria pushed from him, spun about twice, and let her skirt drop to the floor. The lightning outside became more intense, typical of a spring Montana storm. The light outlined her, shining around her and occasionally giving tempting glimpses of the dark fleece patch between her thighs. Tiny drops like the morning dew already dotted that thick bush, and Slocum knew he would never be able to keep himself from the woman.

She was simply too beautiful, too willing—and married. The thought plagued him like a burr under a saddle blanket, but she quickly made him forget it.

Gloria moved back to the bed and lay alongside him. They kissed and explored each other's bodies until Slocum felt as if he were going to explode. She sensed his nearness and moved like a snake over him, her silken flesh slipping on his until she straddled his waist.

"You're about the most beautiful woman I ever saw," Slocum said truthfully.

"Hush," she said. "No talking. Just . . . this." Gloria lifted herself and gripped his fleshy length. She positioned it under her body, then slowly sank down. She sighed deeply as he vanished within her most intimate chamber. Slocum closed his eyes and fought to keep from blowing up like a stick of dynamite. She had ways of stimulating him and she used them. It took all his control to keep from coming like some young buck with his first woman.

Just when Slocum thought he couldn't go on any longer, Gloria slipped off his throbbing length. He looked down and saw her turning around. The curved moons of her ass cheeks gleamed in the light from outside, tempting, beckoning. He sat up, then got his legs under him.

Gloria gripped the brass rail at the foot of the bed as Slocum moved behind her. His hands circled her waist, brushed lightly through the tangle of fleecy fur matted there, then stroked up along her belly. She gasped and sighed with his every touch. When he cupped both her pendulous breasts, she tossed her head and sent a curtain of dark hair back into his face.

The fragrance of her hair spurred him on. Slocum moved closer, his manhood parting her buttocks. He sank deeper and found a carnal oasis surrounding him. This was more than he could take. His hips began swinging back and forth in the ages-old rhythm of a man loving a woman.

Gloria's body sheened with sweat and then she shuddered. Slocum wondered if it was reaction to the storm outside—or one he created within her. She moaned and began shoving her hips back to meet his every stroke. Together they lost all control and strove together for the ultimate pleasure.

Exhausted, Slocum sank back to the bed. He wasn't sure if Gloria had found that ultimate in satisfaction, but he had. She turned and looked positively wolfish.

"More," she demanded. "That was good, but I want more."

Slocum shook his head. He couldn't go on letting his balls do his thinking for him.

"It's not a disputable point. You're married—and not to me."

Gloria laughed and tossed her head like a filly frolicking in the pasture. She lay full-length beside Slocum and put her face close to his. He felt her hot breath, her lush body, the way she moved. He had resolved to make that the last time he made love to her, but his resolve was weakening.

Then he sat bolt upright when he heard what she whispered in his ear.

"What? You're not married to Benbow?"

"No, John, I'm not. Samuel's my brother."

Slocum stared at her, not sure if he believed her or not. Then tiny pieces all fell together and showed him a bigger, more realistic picture.

"You're not English, are you?"

"No," she admitted. "We're from Boston originally. Papa brought us out to Laramie when we were young. Samuel was twelve and I was ten. We've lived in Wyoming most of our lives and have never been to England. But then, the people in Bannack have hardly *heard* of England, so we thought it was safe."

"And pretending to be Englishmen let you poke around without anyone getting suspicious," Slocum said.

"Right. The one thing we've found is that folks tend to clam up when strangers ask a lot of questions—unless they think the people are fools."

"You played the part well," Slocum admitted. "You gave yourselves away with the way you used your guns this afternoon."

"We had to. There wasn't any way I would let you get ventilated," Gloria said. "I'm quite fond of you, John. Really." Her fingers danced lightly over his naked body to convince him. Slocum didn't need convincing. She had already shown him.

"What is it about the road agents you are so intent on finding out?"

Gloria sighed. "They killed our pa. He had gone up to Helena to start a freighting company between South Pass and the coast. Plummer—or those working for him—thought Pa was carrying gold. All he had was a load of furniture that would be worthless to anyone. They might have gotten mad that he carried nothing of value, or he might have tried defending himself. We've never found out—we've never heard from Pa again either. Not even his body has been found."

"That streak of mean runs in your family," Slocum said.

"You've noticed. Samuel is worse than I am, but if I had the goods on Plummer, I'd willingly put the noose around his neck."

"Why not just kill him? You and your brother"—Slocum liked the way that rolled off his tongue—"are good enough with your pistols."

"We want to destroy the whole damned organization!" Gloria flared. "Kill Plummer and Hunter would take over. Kill him and there's Cleveland or Forbes or any of a dozen others. We want the law to eradicate the whole gang!"

"The federal marshal in Helena isn't likely to come after a popular sheriff unless you have Plummer cold, is that it?"

"Yes," she said in a voice so frigid that Slocum felt the temperature in the room drop. "And we will get him. We have found out all the little tricks Plummer uses to rob those along Alder Gulch. We need to know where his headquarters is."

"Road Agent Rock," Slocum said.

"You've been there, seen it? Can you take us there?" Gloria sat up in the bed.

Slocum shook his head. "The canyons are a turny, twisty maze. I got lost twice in there. I need to do some serious exploring, and that's not likely to happen with the road agents so active."

"And so organized. Nothing gets by them."

"Nothing except a British lord and lady," Slocum said.

Gloria grinned. It was feral. "I don't know how much Plummer suspects. I know he and Hunter were both wondering about you."

"It's a dangerous game you're playing. What are you planning to do?" Slocum felt a curious push-pull. He wanted to help the Benbows as much as he wanted to simply get the hell out of Bannack and let Plummer and his gang rob at will.

"The packet you took from the courier this afternoon," Gloria said. "I want to see it."

Slocum hesitated, and he wasn't sure why.

"John, please. The man admitted he was carrying a message. What does it say?"

"Haven't looked." Slocum rolled over and rummaged through his discarded clothing until he found the oilcloth-wrapped packet. Gloria took it from him and eagerly unwrapped it. She scanned the contents.

"Plans!" she crowed. "They are going to waylay three big gold shipments along the Gulch. This will require great coordination on their part—and most of their men. Samuel and I know they don't have more than thirty outlaws in their gang."

"Thirty?" Slocum closed his eyes and lay back. They would be fighting an army—and an army with the local lawmen on their side.

"Look, the ink is smudged here," Gloria said, as if finding a gold mine. "I can alter the date of the shipment. Highwaymen will go after the gold on the wrong day and—"

"And you'll catch them in the act," Slocum finished.

"With federal deputies," she added. "There will be no way they can get out of this trap!"

"There's only one problem," Slocum said.

"What?" she asked.

"How do we get the courier's packet back in the hands of the outlaws so they won't get suspicious?"

Neither of them had an answer to that.

10

Slocum rose before dawn, went to the window, and looked out over Bannack's streets. The rain had subsided sometime after midnight, but he had hardly noticed then. He stretched, his body aching. He hadn't had this much loving in longer than he could remember. Gloria Benbow lay stretched out naked on his bed, a gentle smile on her lovely, sleeping face and looking like a contented cat.

He reflected how apt that comparison was. She could purr one minute and be all claws and teeth the next. He had seen her anger when she spoke of Henry Plummer and his gang and how they had killed her father; yet she had turned into a marvelous bed partner a few seconds later.

She was almost more than he could handle—but Slocum was willing to keep trying, especially now that she had told him she and Samuel Benbow were not married.

A woman like her could make a man mighty happy for a long, long time.

Slocum's attention turned back to the muddy morass of Bannack's streets. The flickering gaslights that hadn't blown out during the storm cast a wan light on the town's soggy buildings, showing a few citizens already up and stirring. They industriously wiped mud from the fronts of their stores and tried to clean the walkways for their customers.

Slocum enjoyed the feel of a town preparing for business when the flash of light off a badge warned him that Henry Plummer might never sleep.

The sheriff strode along the boardwalk in front of a row of saloons, a big stogie clamped between his teeth. The lawman stopped at the edge of the wooden walk and puffed vigorously. Clouds of blue smoke rose and obscured his face for a moment. Then a quick breeze came down the street and revealed his face again. The lawman's eyes were keen, not missing a detail around him.

Slocum glanced at the packet and the forged documents carried by the outlaws' courier. Would the changed date pass Plummer or would the gang leader know immediately he was riding into a trap? Slocum knew the way men like Plummer thought, and he didn't doubt Plummer fit the mold exactly. Money counted for a considerable amount, Slocum thought, but power ruled Plummer absolutely.

He cared less for the gold and what it might buy than for the power it gave him.

Slocum quickly dressed. Gloria continued sleeping peacefully. He saw no reason to rouse her for what might be a cold and lonely vigil. He wanted to follow Henry Plummer and see what the sheriff's routine was like. If an opportunity presented itself, Slocum would slip the courier's oilcloth-wrapped message into the man's hands.

If it didn't, at least Slocum would have gotten to know

Plummer a mite better. That knowledge might save his life later.

Colt stuck into his cross-draw holster, Slocum opened the door and slipped into the hallway. He carefully avoided the creaky floorboards and went downstairs. The clerk had his feet up on the counter, a newspaper resting over his face as he slept. For a moment, Slocum considered taking a lucifer and setting fire to the paper to see what the man might do. He shoved such a notion away. After last night, Slocum was feeling frisky. Perhaps too frisky.

He needed to be cautious around a stone killer like Henry Plummer.

The wind proved colder than Slocum had thought peering out from his hotel window. He turned up his collar and slipped and slid through the thick mud, making his way down the street to where he could follow Plummer. Almost immediately Slocum found himself diving for cover.

Plummer and his chief deputy, Bill Hunter, met in the middle of the street. They argued, and Slocum wasn't sure what it was about. Hunter kept pointing in the direction of the Royal Hotel, but Slocum got no sense that the outlaw wanted to march in and start killing everyone in sight—or just John Slocum.

The sheriff waved Hunter off and sauntered across the sea of mud to a general store. Slocum warily watched as Hunter took his hat off, slapped it hard against his leg in anger, then stalked off in the direction of the town jail. Only then did Slocum follow Plummer. Slocum got to the walk outside in time to see Plummer shove something into his pocket inside the store. Still puffing on his cigar, Plummer came out. He passed Slocum, never knowing he was being spied upon.

For an hour Slocum trailed the sheriff, watching him go into every business along the main street. And in every place the sheriff received a small stack of greenbacks from the owner. The lawman shoved his tribute into his coat pocket and left.

Slocum went into a pharmacy after the sheriff left. The man behind the stained-wood counter looked up, fire in his eyes.

"What can I do for you, mister?" he asked, trying to force civility into his tone. His anger boiled over.

"I'm needing something special," Slocum said, choosing his words carefully.

"Reckon I can fix you up with about any kind of medicine. What ails you?"

"The same thing that ails Sheriff Plummer," Slocum said, staring straight at the pharmacist. "Can you give me what you just gave him?"

"Get the hell out! I pay tribute to that son of bitch so he doesn't burn me out or toss me in jail! I won't pay two of you blood-sucking sons of bitches!" The man reached under the counter and grabbed a hickory stave. He waved it wildly, forcing Slocum from the small shop.

In the street, Slocum quickly walked from the store to avoid being shouted at. He didn't want to draw anyone's attention to himself, especially Henry Plummer's. A crooked smile crossed Slocum's lips. Plummer had it all in Bannack. He robbed the miners and freight companies if they tried to transport their metal to Helena or Nevada City or even Salt Lake City. And he robbed the people in his town by extortion.

"Power," Slocum told himself. Plummer sought power, not the pitiful few dollars he squeezed from the citizens of Bannack. How much longer would the people put up with his ways, Slocum wondered. When the law turned against them, people tended to band together into vigilance committees to take care of their own.

Slocum had seen enough for the moment. He had to decide how to pursue Plummer, for both the Benbows' purpose and for one that was beginning to form in his own mind.

• • •

"He wouldn't suspect me," Samuel Benbow insisted that night. "I can get it back to him."

Slocum shook his head. Across the dinner table he looked from Gloria to her brother and back.

"You don't want to draw such attention to yourselves," Slocum said.

"It's nothing," insisted Benbow. "I'll tell him I found it out on the road as we were returning to town."

"I think John is right," Gloria said. "That's pretty lame. From the way he looks at us, he might know who we are— or at least suspect."

"A man like Plummer suspects everyone," said Benbow. "There's no way he could know why we are here or who we are."

"He doesn't have to," said Slocum. "All he needs to think is that you are a danger to him. A man like that kills people with no more thought than grinding a roach under his heel."

"You have the look of a gunfighter about you, Slocum. Would you face him down, if we can't get the goods on him?" Samuel Benbow's jaw turned firmer and any hint of indolence had long since vanished from his eyes. He was no longer playing the role of an English dandy around Slocum.

"Don't see any reason to, unless he forces my hand. Let me try to work my way into his organization. You and Gloria can fetch the marshal from Helena. Tell him about the three robberies—tell him about the one you changed the date on."

"That's the best evidence we could have," Benbow said. "No one would get hurt during the robbery and we would still catch Plummer red-handed."

"Working from inside the gang is a better way of getting the packet into his hands," Slocum insisted. "Just don't forget to tell your federal marshal that when the shooting starts.''

"John, wait." Gloria caught his arm as he stood to leave. "This is too dangerous."

"Playing with a rattler like Plummer is always dangerous. I'd rest easier knowing you were safe."

Gloria impulsively rose and kissed him quickly, then sat down, blushing. Slocum glanced around the small café to see if anyone noticed her public display. If they had, they made no sign that it had offended them. Slocum figured Gloria had moved quick enough that no one had seen her unseemly actions.

Slocum tipped his hat to Gloria and her brother, then headed into the twilight to find the sheriff. He felt alone for the first time in longer than he could remember. He had come to appreciate Gloria Benbow in a short time. Now it seemed wrong when he left her. Slocum shook his head. Thinking like that could get a man killed.

What he planned on doing required his full attention. Henry Plummer wasn't the kind of man likely to show an instant of remorse when it came to suspecting—or killing.

Slocum searched four saloons before he found the sheriff sitting quietly in the back of the Hangman's Noose Saloon. A shot glass, still filled with whiskey, sat on the table in front of the sheriff. He held it, but made no move to hoist it to his lips.

Slocum sidled up to the bar and watched the curious internal struggle going on in Plummer. Every time Slocum thought the sheriff was going to down the rotgut, Plummer forced his hand away from the glass.

"What's going on?" Slocum asked the barkeep. "Why doesn't he finish his drink and then order another, if he's still got a thirst?"

The barkeep twirled his long handlebar mustache and glanced sideways at the sheriff. His expression told Slocum this wasn't the first time Plummer had played this little game with his whiskey.

"He's one mean drunk, Sheriff Plummer is," the bartender said. "And he knows it. When he's sober, he's polite, even gentle. But drunk? He could whip ten times his weight in mountain men and never break a sweat. He could *kill* them and never notice. Mean clean through, Plummer is."

As Slocum drank slowly, he watched the men coming and going. Many were miners come to town for a little liquid lightning to ease the pain of working long hours in their shafts. Others carried their six-shooters slung low and were looking for a fight.

Slocum saw that this group split about in half. Some took one look at the solitary Henry Plummer and hightailed it. Others nodded in his direction, made arcane symbols in the air, or even went to speak with him a few minutes. These were the members of Plummer's gang and the ones Slocum had to deal with if he wanted to lure Plummer into a trap using the dead courier's packet as bait.

A tall man, thin as a rail, entered the saloon. The hubbub died and all eyes turned to him. The way the skeletal man's finger twitched over the pearl handle of his Colt told Slocum this was one gent looking for a fight. The midnight-black eyes never strayed left or right. They fixed squarely on the seated Sheriff Plummer.

For the first time since Slocum had entered the saloon, Plummer let his hand lift the glass. He downed the liquor in a single gulp. He clicked the glass back onto the stained tabletop and moved his chair a fraction of an inch. Other than this, he showed no emotion.

"I want a word with you, Plummer," the tall man said. His boots clicked as he walked and his silver spurs jangled. Slocum saw he wore cruel Spanish rowels, wheels that would rake and turn bloody in a few minutes the flanks of any horse unlucky enough to seat this rider.

"Evening, Mr. Cleveland," Plummer said. The name brought Slocum up. He remembered Gloria mentioning a gang member named Cleveland.

Cleveland planted his feet wide and moved his coat back from his six-gun.

Slocum turned a bit, getting his hand closer to the ebony butt of his own Colt Navy. If shooting started, he wasn't going to simply watch. But whose side would he take?

"You been cheatin' me again," Cleveland declared. "You owe me a powerful lot of money."

"Now why is that, Mr. Cleveland?" asked Plummer in a deceptively gentle voice. "You do your work, you get paid what's fair. How am I cheating you?"

"You been skimmin' off the top. You keep more 'n your fair share. Hell, your share shouldn't be any different than the rest of us."

"Are you calling me a thief, Mr. Cleveland?" For all the emotion he showed, Henry Plummer might have been asking the time or if Cleveland expected it to rain some more.

"You know what you are, Plummer. You're a low-down, backshooting thief who'd steal pennies off a dead man's eyes."

"Are you calling me out, Mr. Cleveland?" Plummer made no move to stand or free the six-shooter hanging at his side.

"You know I am. We'll have this out once and for all. After I kill you, I'm gonna divvy the entire stash with the others."

"Where do you propose we have this shootout?" asked Plummer.

Slocum blinked and almost missed what happened. Sheriff Plummer spoke in his conversational voice, his six-shooter difficult to draw while he was sitting down. But Slocum had almost forgotten the chance showing of the sheriff's derringer earlier. Plummer drew the small gun and fired into Cleveland's chest before the tall man could so much as begin his draw.

"I am tired of this," Plummer said in an offhand manner.

Cleveland stood like a tall tree in the forest, then toppled with his knees locked rigidly. He crashed into the table next to Plummer.

He slid from the table, dropped to his knees, and stared up at Plummer. "I'm down, Henry. Don't shoot me again."

"Get up," ordered Plummer. Cleveland fought to get to his feet. The sheriff watched emotionlessly, then shoved the derringer into Cleveland's face and fired the second barrel. The round caught Cleveland just under the eye. This time the tall, thin man fell and lay unmoving on the floor.

Plummer knocked open his derringer, ejected the spent casings, and reloaded. The small but deadly gun vanished back into a vest pocket.

Without a word, Plummer went to the next table. He called out, "Barkeep! A whiskey!"

That was all the emotion he showed over cutting down one of his gang. Slocum relaxed, and then tensed again when a gust of wind came through the door. On the night breeze came Bill Hunter and three other deputies. Without a word, they picked up Cleveland's lifeless body and carried it out the rear door into the alley.

Slocum imagined them stripping the body of its valuables, then simply leaving Cleveland's carcass to be stripped by the packs of dogs that roamed Bannack.

After waiting a few minutes for Hunter and his cronies to return, Slocum saw that Plummer was unmoved by the quick gunfight. The man sat and stared at the new shot glass put in front of him.

"Hey, Henry, you up for a friendly game of poker?" called a portly man coming into the saloon. He held out a deck of worn cards. For the first time Slocum could remember, Henry Plummer smiled and motioned the man over. Two others joined them, and Slocum saw his chance.

He downed his whiskey and went to the only empty chair remaining at the table.

"Mr. Slocum," Plummer said, as if noticing him for the first time. Slocum was sure Plummer had known he had been in the saloon since before Cleveland's killing.

"Mind if I join you?" Slocum asked. "It's been a while since I played a game of poker."

"Draw, five-card stud, what's your pleasure?" With that Plummer shut out the portly man and the others, making this a contest between him and Slocum.

"Stud," Slocum said. He pulled up a chair and sat opposite Plummer. The play began slowly, the stakes low. The others at the table sensed the tension between Slocum and Plummer, but pointedly ignored it. Slocum found the forced joviality almost laughable.

Hand by hand the stakes began to increase. Plummer was a cool player, as Slocum had expected. Anyone who could gun down a man and never bat an eye had to be.

"Seems we are approaching table limit," Plummer said as the pot grew. "You've got a pair of kings showing. Me, all I've got is a lonely ace."

Slocum took a quick look at his down card; he had a third king. But he wasn't sure he wanted to win the pot. The courier's packet lay in his coat pocket, weighing heavily.

"You don't seem to be folding," Slocum pointed out. He had not seen Plummer cheating, but he wouldn't put it past the sheriff. The man won, using whatever methods necessary.

"I'm raising. Everything I have, if you have no objection."

Slocum had more than fifty dollars in the pot. With Plummer's raise, there was close to three hundred riding on the turn of the cards.

"Can't match that," Slocum lied, "with only greenbacks, but maybe this might be of interest. It's something

I found out on the road the other day.''

"Is it now?" Plummer's eyebrow rose slowly at the sight of the courier's packet.

"Yesterday, when you came across me out in the canyon," Slocum said.

"Don't imagine this could have simply fallen out of someone's pocket, do you?"

Slocum shrugged. Plummer could come to any conclusion he wanted. All Slocum wanted was to get the forged timetable back into the outlaw's hands. He pushed the courier's packet into the center of the table. From the corners of his eyes Slocum saw the other players at the table exchange confused looks. They didn't understand what Plummer would find valuable enough to match against a huge pile of cash.

"Sorry, Mr. Slocum. It appears you lose." Plummer turned over a second ace, beating the pair of kings Slocum had showing.

"You have anything more hidden away in your hole cards?" asked Slocum.

"Do I need it?" Plummer fixed him with a steely look.

"Reckon not," Slocum said, shoving his winning hand back into the deck.

"You are mighty generous," Plummer allowed. "If you will excuse me." Then he rose and walked from the saloon without a backward glance. He had the packet tucked safely away in his inside coat pocket, the rest of the pot carelessly stuffed into his outer pocket.

"That cleans me out, gents," Slocum said. He pushed back from the table and went to tell the Benbows he had set up the sheriff. All they need do now was fetch the federal marshal and they would catch Plummer red-handed robbing a gold shipment.

Slocum stepped into the night air, sucked in a deep breath, and then crashed forward as someone behind struck him with the butt of a pistol. He fought to get to his feet again. A second blow sent him facedown, unconscious.

11

Sunlight in his eyes made Slocum twist to one side to avoid the brightness. He strained against unseen bonds. Squinting, he opened his eyes a crack to stare at the crisp blue Montana sky dotted with puffy white clouds. He tried shaking his head to clear it, but something inside rattled and hurt.

Slocum held back a moan as he tried to sit up. He was too securely tied down.

Looking around the best he could he saw he was staked out spread-eagle in hard ground. From the elevation of the sun it might be close to noon, which accounted for the glaring light in his eyes. Somewhere on his way to captivity he had lost his hat. From the lack of weight at his waist he knew his six-shooter had been taken by whoever slugged him.

Slocum lay back and pieced together the events the best

he could. He had given the packet with the forged documents to Plummer, then left the saloon. Not paying attention and gloating at his minor victory over the outlaw, he had never heard the owlhoot who had hit him come up from behind. That much was obvious to Slocum. What wasn't as plain was the answer to an important question.

Where was he?

Arching his back and twisting his body, he saw a familiar sight. The huge red rock monolith where the road agents camped was barely visible out of the corner of his eye. He sank back to the hard ground.

Road Agent Rock.

It was as he feared. Plummer wasn't about to simply accept the courier's packet. He wanted more—and he wasn't the sort who would take kindly if he didn't get it straightaway. Slocum remembered too well how Henry Plummer had cut down the tall, thin gunfighter without even blinking.

The derringer in the vest pocket was deadly, but the man who wielded it was a stone killer.

"You're a remarkable fellow," said Plummer's soft, genteel voice. "Not even the flies annoy you. My horse over yonder"—Plummer must have pointed, but Slocum wasn't able to see the sheriff—"is bedeviled by the flies. Little things, hardly big enough to see. But you, Mr. Slocum, you lie there like a lizard sunning himself on a warm rock."

"I'd enjoy it a mite more if I wasn't staked out like this," Slocum said.

Plummer laughed, but it held no humor. The sheriff walked around and stood at Slocum's feet where the bound man could see his captor. Plummer's fingers tapped lightly on the six-gun holstered at his side. He pursed his lips, and finally spoke after thinking on the matter a few seconds.

"What shall we do with you? You present a problem unlike others that have arisen recently."

"I don't aim to be anyone's problem," Slocum said.

"No, that's not true," Plummer contradicted. "I think you aim to be everyone's problem. The way you carry that Colt of yours, its worn butt, the way you talk, the way you never miss anything going on around you, all that spells trouble in my book, Mr. Slocum. You are a very dangerous man, but I don't know where you belong in this picture."

Slocum said nothing. He figured to let Plummer get to the point. Only then would he know how big the mess he had landed in might be.

"Why did you give me the courier's packet?"

"I lost it fair and square in the poker game. I thought it might be valuable. It must have been. You staked two hundred in greenbacks against it."

"A lie, Mr. Slocum. Don't lie or I'll cut your tongue out and stuff it down your throat." Plummer was not joking.

"I wanted to ride with your gang."

"Ah," said Plummer, "a spark of truth. Or is it? How do you know anything about 'my gang,' as you call it?"

"Everyone knows how hard it is to move gold along Alder Gulch. It takes a big gang and a smart boss to sew things up as tight as they are here."

"That does not implicate me, or does it?" Plummer frowned. "My deputies. You must have connected Hunter or Forbes with a robbery."

Slocum let the sheriff come to his own conclusions. As long as the Benbows weren't mentioned, Slocum thought Gloria and her brother might be safe. The instant Plummer suspected they were on his trail, he would kill them.

"That doesn't say anything about the packet. Where did you get it? Did you kill the courier?"

"No, you did." Slocum saw surprise spread on Plummer's face. The sheriff's expression fell back into a poker face almost immediately.

"A curious thing to tell me. Are you saying the man I

shot yesterday out here in the canyons was my own courier?''

"You didn't know?" This took Slocum by surprise. He tugged a mite more at the ropes around his wrists. He would never get free on his own.

"Perhaps I was too quick, but I thought he was being taken prisoner by a federal marshal. It seems I was wrong. When we rode up, I did not identify him as a courier. He was a recruit and had responsibilities I knew nothing about given him by his lieutenant.''

Slocum began to understand more fully how Plummer ran his gang. Gloria had said it was organized like a military unit. Some subordinate took care of moving messages up and down the Gulch to Plummer's far-flung highwaymen. He assigned a subordinate to take care of this and knew nothing of who was actually sent on each mission.

"I could have destroyed the packet.''

"That would have meant nothing to me," Plummer said.

"You were mighty anxious to get it during the poker game," Slocum pointed out. This game of cat-and-mouse was wearing on him. He wanted the outlaw to either kill him or let him go.

"It contains information I find very useful—and profitable," Plummer said. "Do you know what is inside that packet?''

"Information about gold shipments," Slocum said, seeing no point in lying. Plummer would never believe he hadn't looked in it. Otherwise, how would Slocum have known how to use it so enticingly? "I might have used it to my own advantage, but I gave it back to you. I want to ride with you.''

"That poses a problem, Mr. Slocum. There's no room in the gang right now.''

Slocum laughed harshly. "You must have thirty or forty men in the gang. And you killed the courier. That ought to leave one opening. And what about Cleveland? You killed him too.''

''Cleveland got greedy. He thought he ought to be leader of this fine group. He was wrong.'' Plummer stared at Slocum. The sheriff reached under his coat and whipped out a large-bladed knife. He cocked it back next to his ear and then let it fly. Slocum never flinched as it cartwheeled through the air toward him. The heavy knife sliced the bonds on his right wrist. In a flash, Slocum retrieved the knife and cut the remaining ropes.

He tossed the knife back to Plummer. The blade vanished as quickly as it had appeared.

''Glad to be in your gang,'' Slocum said.

''It's not that easy, Slocum,'' Plummer said, his voice cold. ''You are on probation for a job or two, just to be certain we can trust you.''

Slocum glanced over his shoulder. A dozen of Plummer's gang stood behind him, between him and Road Agent Rock. If he made a wrong move, a dozen six-shooters would empty their loads into his back.

''Why isn't Plummer riding with us?'' Slocum asked. The deputy, Buck Stinson, turned in the saddle and fixed Slocum with a cold stare.

''You don't go askin' questions like that. The boss don't come out on jobs. And you never mention him by name. Never. If you do . . .'' Stinson drew his thumb across his throat in a graphic gesture.

Slocum chafed at the wait. They had left Road Agent Rock and ridden hard—and in circles—for almost two days, finding a promontory looking over the Alder Gulch Road leading out of Nevada City. He wished he knew if this robbery was the one Gloria had faked in the courier's packet. If it was, they would find themselves up to their ears in federal marshals before they knew it.

If it wasn't, Slocum was going to be throwing lead at

men determined to protect their gold shipment—and all for nothing. Henry Plummer would never give him so much as an ounce of gold dust for his efforts.

Slocum wished he could slip away from Stinson, but the deputy kept him in sight constantly. Slocum wasn't even allowed to take a leak without one of the road agents nearby to make sure he didn't hightail it. His fingers closed around the butt of his Colt, but he knew how feeble the weapon was with only five rounds in its cylinder.

They had taken all his ammo—and six men rode behind him. Even if he had the best streak of luck and made a kill with every shot, he would still be at the mercy of the remaining outlaw. And Slocum wasn't kidding himself into thinking he would even wing five of them if he started shooting. Stinson kept an eagle eye on him. The slightest muscle twitch the deputy didn't like and Slocum knew he was dead.

He figured Plummer's orders were to the point: kill Slocum if he gives you any trouble.

"You know what you're supposed to do," Stinson told him. "You ride on out into the road and just stand there. The driver might rein back to see what's wrong. Maybe not. It don't matter. All we need is for the driver and shotgun messenger to be lookin' the wrong way when we ride down behind them."

"There's not much I can do with only five shots," Slocum said.

"You don't have to do anything but stand there and look purty," Stinson said with a curt laugh. "We'll do the actual robbin'."

Slocum tried to remember the details of the three robberies outlined in the courier's packet. He failed. Was this the one Gloria had altered? Or was it another robbery?

"No need to get worked up, Slocum," said Stinson. "You ever robbed a stagecoach before?"

Slocum snorted in disgust. Stinson was trying to tell him how to rob a stage.

"Don't matter," Stinson said. "There's the signal." In the distance a mirror reflected sunlight in a distinct pattern.

Slocum wondered how many others Plummer had taking part in the robbery. Stinson had five, not counting Slocum, with him. The lookout was another. And others? The Bannack sheriff took no chances.

"Get on down there, Slocum. Don't get too anxious now." Stinson laughed and the others joined him. They were drawing up their bandannas to hide their faces, but Slocum had been told not to do this. He would be recognized by the driver and guard and any passengers and would find his face on a new set of wanted posters.

Unless Stinson had orders to kill everyone.

Slocum had no doubt that he would be included in that slaughter, if Plummer wanted no eyewitnesses left behind to complicate his life.

He picked his way down the trail until he reached the spot in the road they had marked with a stack of stones. Slocum heard a six-gun cocking but he didn't see the gunman. A glint off a rifle barrel told of another sniper hidden in the rocks. That meant the five riding with Stinson were only a part of the gang sent out for the robbery. This made Slocum increasingly uneasy.

Even if they rode into an ambush set up by the federal marshal in Helena, there was enough firepower to shoot out of any trap.

Slocum reined his horse back and wheeled it about to stare down the road. He heard the clatter of the stagecoach long before he saw it. He had the sensation of movement all around him, as in the desert at twilight. Animals stirred, predators hunted, and prey died. And all of it was unseen.

The stage rounded a bend in the road. The driver used his whip to keep the six-horse team struggling up a long, steep grade. Slocum admired the way Plummer had set up the robbery. The driver and team would be occupied with the steep incline, not paying attention to anyone thinking about robbery. The shotgun messenger saw Slocum right away and tugged at the driver's sleeve.

Slocum took off his hat and waved it back and forth to draw their attention. He took a second to look left and right. Stinson and the others were in position for their attack. Slocum's breath came faster and his heart raced. The robbery was going to happen no matter what he did. Trying to warn the driver only played into the trap.

Which was exactly what Henry Plummer would have wanted.

"Git out of the road! We'll drive right on over you!" shouted the guard. Slocum knew different. The driver had already dug his heels into the box and pulled back hard to slow the team. It didn't require much effort on his part slowing them. They were tuckered out from the hard pull uphill.

"What do you want, mister?" shouted the driver.

"To rob you," Slocum shouted. He saw Stinson give the signal. The five road agents riding with the deputy rode onto the road behind the stagecoach and came up on either side, guns drawn.

The shotgun messenger twigged to the trap and yelled a warning. He spun in the box and let loose with both barrels of his shotgun. One outlaw exploded as the heavy buckshot ripped through him. Then all hell was let loose.

Stinson and his partners opened up on the guard. The man danced about as slug after slug ripped through him. Slocum saw Stinson empty one six-shooter and then draw another. He emptied that into the shotgun messenger and reached for his rifle.

"Wait, I'm giving up!" the driver cried. He threw down the reins and his hands shot skyward. This only made him a better target for the outlaws. Four rounds thudded into his chest as Slocum watched.

"Wait, he was surrendering!" Slocum shouted.

"Shut up," snapped Stinson. "The son of a bitch let his guard kill Castle." He used his rifle to indicate the pieces of outlaw lying in the road. "Nobody gets away with that."

Another of the road agents jumped to the ground and jerked open the door. He used his gun to gesture to the passengers to get out of the coach.

Slocum was worried the outlaws would kill the three men and woman riding in the stagecoach. Stinson jumped from his horse and caught the edge of the driver's box, pulling himself up. He reached down in the foot well and grunted as he pulled out the strongbox. He heaved and sent it sailing through the air to land at the passengers' feet.

"Take care of that, will you, Slocum?" Stinson called. His face was obscured by his mask, but Slocum knew Stinson was grinning. Calling him by name sealed his fate if any of the passengers lived to tell the law about the robbery. Two men dead meant the stagecoach company would post a big reward. A lost gold shipment angered miners and refiners.

The only name anyone could attach to the crime would be that of Slocum. If they lived.

Slocum had no qualms about shooting down a man who needed it. He had done more than his share of killing over the years, starting with a carpetbagger judge and his hired gun back in Calhoun, Georgia. If Henry Plummer had been standing in front of him right now, Slocum was sure he wouldn't have any regrets about cutting the sheriff down. But killing unarmed men and women caught in his craw.

"You going to get the gold out of the box, Stinson?" Slocum called loud enough to anger the deputy. Slocum played a dangerous game. If he pushed Stinson too much, the deputy would never hesitate to kill the three men and the woman standing with their hands raised. But Slocum had no other way of telling Stinson he didn't approve of the way the outlaw was conducting the robbery.

"You do it," Stinson said. Not naming Slocum again let Slocum breathe a little easier. Maybe none of the passengers had heard any names being called out.

Slocum dropped down, using his horse to shield himself from the two passengers nearest him. He drew up his bandanna before moving away. He drew his Colt, aimed, and fired. The bullets ricocheted off the padlock. One of the road agents yelped and grabbed his arm. A piece of flying lead had winged him. Slocum ignored his angry curses and fired again. This slug tore off the padlock. Slocum opened the box and caught his breath.

Gold.

This was what all the bother was about.

"I'll take that," Stinson said. He hefted the bags of gold dust into his own saddlebags. "Get the belongings from them." Stinson jerked his thumb in the direction of the passengers.

Slocum simply stood and let the other road agents search the men and take their wallets and watches. None of them wore any jewelry worth stealing. Slocum saw the woman glaring at him. He appreciated her spirit but knew it would get her in big trouble if she tried fighting back.

One outlaw stopped in front of her. Slocum reached out and put his hand on the man's shoulder.

"Let her be. We don't need to rob women." Slocum had only three rounds left in his Colt Navy, but he could put them to good use if the outlaw pressed the matter.

"The boss says everyone. That includes her." The road agent sounded as if he eagerly anticipated searching the woman.

"Not a woman," Slocum said in a steely voice. This certainty caused the road agent to back off. The road agent turned from side to side, imploring his partners to come to his aid. They had heard Slocum's tone and weren't inclined to cross him.

Confidence had accomplished what bullets couldn't have.

"Ma'am," Slocum said, touching the brim of his hat. She did not look as relieved as she did angry. He hoped she kept her mouth shut. Stinson was likely to cut loose and kill her and the other passengers if she put up any protest.

"Let's get on out of here. We have what we came for," Buck Stinson said, swinging into the saddle. For a moment, he stared down at Slocum, his six-shooter wavering. The deputy worked over what he had been ordered to do; Slocum wasn't sure how it was going until Stinson motioned for Slocum to mount.

Slocum wasn't sure if he was relieved or not as he rode surrounded by the road agents, heading back to their hideout.

12

"We're going in circles," Slocum complained. They had ridden the better part of the afternoon through the winding canyons surrounding Road Agent Rock, and he knew Stinson intended to get him confused by the meandering, just as he had on their way to the robbery. Rather than play along, Slocum decided he had nothing to lose by getting it out in the open.

"Orders," Buck Stinson said.

"You always follow orders?"

"Always," Stinson said angrily. Slocum wondered at the wrath boiling up from within the deputy. Did he resent Henry Plummer and his power or was it something else? He might resent being stuck with a new recruit he might have to kill—or not kill, should Slocum prove himself of value to the gang.

"It took two days getting to where we robbed the stage-coach," Slocum said. "There seems to be a more direct route back to the big rock."

"You know it?" Stinson shoved his jaw out belligerently. Slocum had a passing fancy of reaching over and hitting the man as hard as he could. He knew better than to anger Stinson, though. With ten road agents riding along behind, he would never get more than a few yards down the canyon before they shot him in the back.

Even grabbing the deputy and using him as a shield seemed useless. From the way the other road agents talked among themselves, any individual life was worthless. And shooting Stinson might give one of them a chance to move up in the gang. A lieutenant's job carried more power than simply riding along and being told what to do, like some buck private in the cavalry.

"Can't say that I do, but you must," Slocum replied. "I am just getting tuckered out riding in circles. I say let's get on back to the rock so we can get some grub and rest." Slocum reined back and stopped. He decided not to ride even a single pace farther unless Stinson gave in. If he didn't make his stand now, he was never going to be able to do it later on. This was his best chance, and he was taking it.

"He's right, Buck. My butt is hurtin' from all the ridin'. There was no reason we had to take so long gettin' out toward Nevada City. We coulda—"

"Shut up, Curly," snapped Stinson. He glared at the bald man with such anger Slocum thought Stinson might actually throw down on his partner. "We do what we're told."

"Curly's right," Slocum said, driving a wedge between the deputy and the others. "Or doesn't he get a say-so either?"

"Now you listen up, Slocum," started Stinson. Then he clamped his mouth shut when he saw the expressions on the rest of the outlaws. They sided with Slocum. Some even had their hands resting on their gun butts. Stinson was smart enough to know he would have a rebellion on his hands if he didn't make the right decision—fast.

"We take that trail over yonder," the deputy said, pointing down a branching canyon with high, steep walls. "We'll be at the rock by sundown."

Slocum smiled as he rode. He had backed the outlaw down, and had made an enemy as a result. But he had nothing to lose. He figured Henry Plummer wasn't going to let him live much longer if even a hint of Gloria and Samuel Benbow's plan came to the sheriff's ears.

Slocum might be cut down even if Plummer heard nothing of the plot to bring in federal marshals. Plummer was the kind of man who killed for the pure pleasure of it. The way he had gunned down Cleveland showed that he had no shred of mercy in his character.

"I'm glad you spoke up, Slocum," Curly said. "Don't know what's got into Buck. He's usually friendlier than this."

Slocum shrugged it off. He figured to let the others do the talking. The more he listened the better off he would be.

"You done a good enough job back there. Don't understand why Buck was so all-fired het up on killin' the passengers," Curly rambled on. "The driver and that shotgun messenger, now, they deserved it. They ought never to have tried to fight back that way. We done robbed 'nuff stagecoaches along the Gulch so's they'd know what to do. Fact is, we kill most all the drivers and guards, but hardly ever the passengers. How could they ever identify us?"

"Looks as if the boss is here," Slocum said, indicating Plummer's horse.

"That means we get paid right away. Whoopeee!" Curly shouted. The man put his spurs to his horse's flanks and raced off toward Road Agent Rock. Slocum followed with the rest of the outlaws at a more sedate pace. His horse was tired from picking her way through the rocky terrain. When he reached the fire where Plummer held court, Slocum swung from the saddle and tethered his horse nearby.

"Curly reports you did just fine, Slocum," Plummer said, eyeing Slocum closely. "Now Buck's story is a lot different."

"Buck doesn't much like me," Slocum allowed.

"We'll talk that over in a spell," Plummer said. "Bring me the gold." This was greeted with cheers. They all watched as Plummer carefully weighed the gold dust and made meticulous notations in a small book recording the take.

"When do we get our cut?" Slocum asked.

"You don't," Stinson said gruffly.

"None of us gets a cut of this robbery," Curly explained. "We'll get paid, though."

Slocum watched as Plummer carefully unrolled greenbacks from a thick wad and paid each of the outlaws taking part. Men like Curly received fifty dollars. Buck Stinson got one hundred. Slocum tried to figure how much gold dust had been taken, and decided Plummer's cut amounted to more than half. Worse, the greenbacks the sheriff passed out as pay for the job were all issued on a local bank. They were worthless if any of the men tried spending the paper money more than a few miles down the road.

The men greeted a case of whiskey brought from Bannack with more whoops of glee. They set to drinking. Slocum accepted a bottle and sipped at the fiery rotgut. Plummer certainly didn't waste any of his money on good liquor for his men.

Stinson and Hunter stood to one side, arguing. Occasional glances in Slocum's direction told him the subject of their argument. Slocum wondered if Hunter was taking his part, because he knew Stinson never would. He ambled over to Henry Plummer and looked down at the handsome sheriff.

"Where's my cut? Even if it's worthless scrip, I figure I ought to be paid for the risks I took."

"Oh?" One of Plummer's eyebrows arched.

Slocum said nothing. Curly joined him and said, "It's true, Boss. He done everything just as he was told. It wasn't his fault the driver and guard decided to put up a fight."

"I understand he prevented Mr. Stinson from completing the robbery as he saw fit. He refused a direct order."

"I wouldn't let Buck shoot down a woman," Slocum said. "The men were unarmed, but I've done worse in my day."

"I am sure," Plummer said, amused.

"But there was no call to try killing a woman."

"A Georgia sentiment. A Southern gentlemen. How refreshing."

"The money," Slocum demanded. He cared nothing for the paltry payment. He wanted to force Plummer into a decision so he would know where he stood with the gang.

"Very well, Slocum. Here you are. Twenty-five dollars."

"That's half what the others got," Slocum pointed out. He heard Curly suck in his breath, knowing a challenge when he heard one.

"Your apprenticeship is over, Slocum. The next time you'll receive full pay," Plummer said.

Slocum nodded once, turned, and walked away. He had done as good as he was likely to with the leader of these highwaymen. Forcing Plummer to give him something made him one of the gang now. Maybe not a full member, but Curly would pass it around that their boss had accepted Slocum—and over Buck Stinson's objections.

Rejoining the others, Slocum appeared to attack his whiskey with a vengeance. He spilled more onto the thirsty dirt than he dribbled down his gullet. All the while he kept his eyes fixed on Henry Plummer. The man tallied up columns of numbers, smiled, and then tucked the book into an inner coat pocket. Plummer hefted the take from the robbery and walked along the edge of the huge red monolith.

"Hold this for me, Curly?" Slocum shoved his half-empty bottle into the man's hands. "I got to go make a call of nature."

"Don't expect all of it to be here when you get back, Slocum," Curly warned. He alternated drinking between his bottle in his right hand and Slocum's in the left.

"I'll make it fast," Slocum said. He walked quickly, swallowed by the shadows. He avoided one sentry posted high up on the red rock and trailed Henry Plummer into the darkness. He followed more by sound than seeing. The occasional crunch of boot heel on gravel or the grunting as the man lugged the heavy bags of gold dust kept Slocum on the path.

Slocum wanted to find where Henry Plummer stashed the gold. If he could locate it, he might be a rich man. This gang had been terrorizing the Alder Gulch miners for years.

And the gang members sure as hell hadn't been getting their fair share. Somehow, Plummer kept them happy with only a few pieces of bank scrip worth more as toilet paper.

Something warned Slocum to take cover. He fell face-down on the ground and lay unmoving as two men sneaked up behind him.

"Are you sure, Buck?" said Hunter's voice.

"He left the party. Where else would that cayuse head but after the boss?" Buck Stinson sounded even angrier than ever. Slocum wondered if the three—Plummer, Stinson, and Hunter—divvied the real booty among themselves. Or if the sheriff simply promised the division and the two deputies expected it as their due. Later.

Wiggling slightly, Slocum got behind a fallen log, mostly rotted and filled with termites. It still gave him a moment's shelter as the two outlaws stalked by.

Slocum remembered he had only a couple of rounds left in his six-shooter. He needed to get a source of ammo before taking on any of them. A couple of rounds were not enough to cut down both Stinson and Hunter.

Worse, killing them would alert Plummer that his suspicions about the newcomer were correct. Slocum wouldn't last five minutes with the entire band of outlaws after him. He hated to quit when he was close to finding where Plummer hid his ill-gotten gold, but he had no choice. Plummer couldn't lug it too far into the mountains from here, Slocum decided. He knew the general direction and that would have to do. For the moment.

He slipped back, pulled a few thorns from his belly, then returned to the party. Curly had finished both bottles and was dancing around the fire like some kind of demented Indian. The bald outlaw whooped and hollered and carried on.

If Gloria had fetched the marshal and his deputies and brought them into the mountains, Slocum doubted it would have been possible to miss this camp. The loud shouts, the bonfires, everything about the camp would draw the lawmen from Helena like a lodestone. Since the sentries had called out no warning, Slocum figured the marshals would be coming some other time. But when?

He wished he knew.

"Slocum, you want to play some high-low?" Curly staggered over, his greenbacks clutched in his hand. "I can't buy a bucket of spit with this. I need to win more."

"You saw what the boss paid me," Slocum said. He reached into his pocket and pulled out the twenty-five dollars. "I can't match your roll."

"Don't matter," Curly said. He sat heavily, his legs curled in front of him. "I got a deck." He pulled it from his shirt pocket. Greasy fingers had long since smeared the pasteboards, making the cards almost unreadable. Curly dealt a few out and stared at them, fighting to focus his bloodshot eyes.

"What do you say, Slocum? We can get a lot more into

the game. Hey, you guys, get your asses over here. I'm gonna play cards. Me and Slocum are gonna play.''

A few drifted over, more to watch than play.

"Go on, Curly," urged one outlaw, a young man hardly twenty, if Slocum had to guess. "Play some Indian poker with him. That's about your best game."

"All right," Curly said, slurring his words and wobbling slightly. "You know how to play?"

Slocum nodded curtly. He had no desire to play cards, especially with a man as drunk as Curly. That only led to trouble. He figured he could lose the twenty-five dollars he had received from Plummer and that would be the end of it.

"Here," Curly said, dealing one card to Slocum and one to himself. With a quick movement, Curly lifted his card and held it against his forehead where he couldn't see it. Slocum picked up his and duplicated the effort, not seeing his own card.

The one Curly held was a six of clubs. Slocum knew he had a good chance of having a higher card, but everyone in the circle knew his and Curly's cards. From their reaction, he guessed his was lower.

"A dollar," Slocum said. He anted. "And a dollar to make it interesting."

Slocum was right. He had drawn a five of diamonds. But the next hand he could not lose. Curly had a deuce. Unless he also had a deuce he would win. Betting heavily, he won twenty from Curly.

The drunk turned surly.

"You ain't cheatin', are you, Slocum?" the man accused.

"They're your cards," Slocum said. "And everyone's watching us. There's no way I could be hustling you."

"It was fair, Curly," said one of the others. He subsided when Curly glared at him. Slocum saw that Curly shared a trait with Henry Plummer. Sober, he was a decent enough man. Drunk, he turned into a cantankerous and dangerous hombre.

"One more hand. You're luck's bound to turn," Slocum said, trying to encourage the drunk without antagonizing him. He had watched how Curly dealt from the deck and decided the cards had been shaved. In his current drunken state, Curly could never deal the cards he wanted, but that didn't stop him from trying.

"Slocum, the man's cheating you," someone warned.

"I trust him," Slocum said, knowing Curly was doing his drunken best to cheat him. He lifted his card and held it against his forehead as he studied Curly's card. Curly had drawn a four.

Slocum figured his own card had to be a deuce or trey. If he was hustling a mark, that was the way he would work it. Slocum was supposed to think he could not lose and bet heavily. Since he wanted nothing more than to be out of the game, Slocum obliged.

"Let's make this interesting," he said. "I'll bet all I have." Slocum dropped the twenty-five he had received for the robbery plus the other money he had already won off Curly.

"Done," the outlaw said. They lowered their cards and showed them at the same time.

Slocum went cold inside. If Curly had been trying to cheat, he was damned poor at it. Slocum held a seven. He had won easily.

"You been hustlin' me, Slocum. I don't abide by that."

"You dealt," Slocum pointed out, but he saw logic meant nothing.

"You musta slipped in a card when I wasn't lookin'." Curly pushed to his feet, his hand hovering over his six-gun. "Get up, Slocum. I'm callin' you out, you no-account card cheat."

"If you think I was cheating—and I wasn't—here, take it all." Slocum pushed the money toward Curly.

"That proves it! He's backin' down. He *was* cheatin'! I don't abide no card cheats."

Slocum rose, trying to figure a way out of killing Curly. The other road agents stood in lines on either side of the men, enjoying the spectacle. Slocum saw money changing hands as bets were made. He doubted many were betting on him. If he killed Curly, he would end up a buzzard bait in a flash.

"Curly, I—" Slocum never got any further. The drunken outlaw's hand went for his six-shooter. Slocum reacted from years of instinct. His hand whipped across, grabbed his Colt Navy in the cross-draw holster, pulled back, and fired. His bullet took Curly smack in the heart. The outlaw had barely cleared leather. Curly's hand tensed, and he squeezed the trigger, sending the slug into his own leg.

But it didn't matter. He had died the instant Slocum's bullet ripped through his chest. Like a marionette with its strings cut, Curly sank to the ground.

"He forced me," Slocum said. He tried to remember how many rounds he had left. He was afraid it was only one—one against dozens of road agents moving closer around him.

13

John Slocum backed away, a cold calmness settling on him. He had felt this way a few times before when it looked as if death were unavoidable. Each of those times he had—sometimes narrowly—escaped a cold berth in the ground.

But now he had only one or two rounds left to stand off two dozen men—or more. He faced them squarely and without a show of fear. Slocum knew any panic on his part would only cause them to kill him instantly. With any luck at all, he could scramble up onto Road Agent Rock and take out a sentry, then get to his horse. In the darkness he might evade the outlaws.

Or he could sprout wings and fly away. Either looked equally probable.

"You killed Curly," one said. Then the outlaw chuckled. The chuckle spread, and soon the road agents were laughing uproariously. Slocum lowered his six-shooter and tucked it back into his holster. No matter what happened, the round or two left would never hold back the wall of mean facing him.

"You're a cool one, Slocum," another outlaw called. "You buy the next round?"

"Sure, why not?" Slocum said, not certain what was meant. Like vultures the men swooped down on the poker pot left where Slocum had dropped it in the dirt. The outlaws passed the money around among themselves, then two left. The few minutes they were gone were tense ones for Slocum. Then he relaxed.

The outlaws dragged back two more cases of whiskey. Where they had been or why it took money to get them, Slocum didn't know. Maybe Henry Plummer ran his own tavern and charged high prices for the tarantula juice. Whatever the explanation, the men gathered around him, slapping him on the back and finally accepting him as one of their own.

Slocum even took a long pull on a bottle shoved into his hand. He choked on the powerful firewater. He pulled the bottle from his lips and held it high.

"Drink up, gents. The liquor's on me!"

And suddenly it was. From a half-dozen nearby bottles came a torrent of the alcohol. Slocum sputtered some more and laughed. He wasn't going to be shot down like a dog. They welcomed him for killing one of their own number. It didn't make a lot of sense but if he had to pass some initiation, this might have been it.

"What's going on?" demanded Hunter, pushing through the crowd. He stepped over Curly and planted himself squarely in front of Slocum.

"He drew first," Slocum said. "It was self-defense. Ask any of my friends." He made a point of indicating the whole gang.

"It's true, Bill. Curly was drunker 'n a skunk. He

throwed down on Slocum. Never seen a man what moved like Slocum. Fast, smooth, accurate. He's a hell of gunman!''

This set off a new round of cheers and toasts. More liquor went down their already well-lubricated throats. Slocum silently held out his bottle to Hunter, daring Plummer's lieutenant to join in the celebration. A curious smile wrinkled Hunter's lips. He took the bottle and downed a hefty slug of the poisonous fluid.

''You're all right, Slocum. I just wish I could remember where I saw you before.''

''Try the wanted posters,'' Slocum said, trying to give the deputy a logical place to hang his suspicions. If he ever connected Slocum with the man he had chased through the canyons and had placed a hundred-dollar reward on, Slocum knew he wouldn't last any longer than an icicle in the hot summer sun.

''Might be,'' Hunter said, taking another drink. He passed the bottle to another outlaw, then drifted into the crowd. Slocum watched him go to the edge of the gang, where he talked again with Buck Stinson. The two deputies didn't argue this time, but there was no agreement between them either.

Slocum guessed Stinson still wanted to put a bullet through his face. Whether Hunter or Plummer or the rousing cheers from the others in the gang stopped Stinson couldn't be fathomed. Slocum was simply happy to have found some camaraderie with the thieves.

The festivities lasted until almost dawn. Slocum collapsed on his bedroll, not sleeping but not quite awake either. He came fully alert when boots approached. He rolled onto his back and stared up at Henry Plummer. The handsome sheriff smiled. Slocum wished he wouldn't. The smile made him look like a wolf sizing up dinner.

''Get your gear, Slocum. We're going into town. I have a job for you. And when you finish it, I'll introduce you to the others as a full member of our gang.''

''I'll get to learn the secret passwords and handshakes?'' Slocum asked.

''All that and more. I'm always looking for sharp operators who can hold their own. You were tossed into a lake with a lot of snapping turtles. You came out just fine. I like that—I *need* that in a lieutenant.''

''You're moving me up in rank mighty fast,'' Slocum said, gathering his blanket.

''I didn't say you were going to be promoted without the rest of the initiation. What you have to do is not going to be easy, not by half. But it is necessary.'' The way Plummer smiled put Slocum on guard.

''What's the job? A bank? A freight wagon? Wells Fargo shipment?''

''Get saddled. We're heading out of camp in a few minutes.'' Plummer spun and walked off, greeting a few of the early risers. Most of the men would come to later with splitting headaches, never knowing their boss had even been in camp. That any were stirring at this early hour told Slocum how well organized Plummer's gang was. They might frolic into the night, but enough remained sober to fight off even a troop of cavalry.

Slocum didn't immediately fetch his horse and saddle. He knelt beside Curly's unused bedroll. Slocum poked through the debris left by the man he had killed. He heaved a sigh of relief when he found enough ammunition for his Colt Navy to put him back in business.

Sitting, Slocum knocked out the cylinder and quickly reloaded. Five minutes passed, and then he was striding along with a usable pistol gently banging at his left side. Six rounds wouldn't mean much in a real fight, but it made him feel better for the moment. He had enough firepower to kill Plummer, Hunter, *and* Buck Stinson.

Only the sheriff sat astride his horse, waiting patiently for Slocum.

"What took you so long?" Plummer demanded, putting the lie to his complacent appearance. Something rankled the sheriff in a big way. It simply didn't show up until Slocum poked a little.

"I had to say good-bye to all my good friends," Slocum said wryly. To his surprise, Plummer laughed.

"You have a certain ironic good humor about you, Slocum. It surprises me. And reminds me not to underestimate you."

"If I'm going to be your right-hand man, there's no need to worry about that, is there?"

Henry Plummer turned more dour. Then the sly smile came back to his face. Slocum was reminded of a cat stalking a sparrow. Deathly quiet would be followed by a surge of muscle, a rush, and then a shower of feathers and blood.

"Get your bandanna up. Cover your eyes so we can ride out of here."

"I'm not allowed to see how we got here?"

"Of course not. The hideout is a closely guarded secret. When you're a full member of the gang, then you'll be shown how to get here from town. It seems Mr. Stinson made a mistake in not taking a more roundabout route reaching the rock coming back from the robbery, but everyone makes a mistake now and then."

"No mistake. You can trust me."

"Yes, of course," said Plummer, indicating by his tone he did not trust Slocum at all. "Your bandanna."

The sheriff waited until Slocum had it in place. Slocum heard a whish but did not move. He guessed Plummer had drawn his knife and lashed it about in front of his face, testing to see if Slocum could see.

"Just sit there and enjoy the ride," Plummer said. Slocum's horse lurched and started off. Slocum tried to keep track of the turnings by the way the sun warmed his face or side or back, but he quickly lost all track of this as

Plummer doubled back, circled, and did everything he could to confuse Slocum.

Even a homing pigeon would have grown bewildered by the constant retracing of the trail. But Slocum knew he would return to Road Agent Rock. The thought of a huge pile of gold nuggets and bags of stolen gold dust kept rising to taunt him. Better that *he* spend that lovely metal than let Henry Plummer enjoy his ill-gotten gains.

Sometime around noon, Plummer halted.

"Take off the blindfold," the sheriff ordered. Slocum blinked at the bright light, then saw the Bannack city limits sign. He settled the bandanna around his neck to soak up some of the sweat running down his face. The spring was turning to summer with ferocious speed.

"What do you want me to do? Rob your own bank?"

"Hardly," said Plummer without a hint of expression on his face. "I want you to kill your employers, the Benbows."

For a moment Slocum felt as if he had been dropped from a tall mountain.

"Is there a problem shooting them down?" asked Plummer.

"What's the reason?"

"I don't need to give you a reason," Plummer snapped. "If you need one, it is because I have ordered you to do it. Kill them and you're in the gang. Don't kill them and you will be hunted down like a dog and killed yourself."

Slocum glanced around and saw Bill Hunter and Buck Stinson down the street. Each had a pair of deputies with him.

"How do I know you won't have me kill the English folks and then throw me in jail for murder?"

"I could throw you in jail for robbing the stagecoach and killing the driver and guard," said Plummer. "That would solve many problems for me and keep the federal marshal at bay a while longer."

"All right," Slocum said, coming to a quick decision. "I'll do it, if it means being an equal member in the gang."

"Equal, with great prospects for advancement," Plummer promised. Slocum couldn't tell if a note of irony hung on those words.

"When do you want it done?"

"Right away, Slocum. And don't tarry. For some reason, Mr. Stinson has not taken a fancy to you."

Slocum urged his horse forward and rode straight to the Royal Hotel. He slid from the saddle and paused at the lobby door. Across the street stood two deputies watching him like hawks. Slocum entered and went to the room clerk. For once the man wasn't snoring.

"I need to talk to Lord Benbow right away."

"Sorry, him and his missus aren't in right now. They left an hour ago, sayin' something about enjoyin' the quaint pleasures of our small hamlet." The clerk frowned. "I thought a hamlet was a little pig."

"A half serving of ham at breakfast," Slocum said, thinking furiously. He left the hotel and started for the café where he and the Benbows had eaten before. He hoped he could find them fast. He doubted Stinson would give him much time to perform his task. Slocum needed all the time he could spare for what had to be done.

At the café door, Slocum paused and looked around the dim, smoky interior. At the rear sat Samuel Benbow and his sister. Gloria spotted him and waved. Slocum hurried over and sat in a third chair.

"John, where have you been?" asked Gloria.

"There's no time for jawing," Slocum said. "I've come to kill you."

14

"Hunter is at the window," Gloria said in a low voice.

Slocum appeared not to hear. He grabbed Samuel Benbow by the frilly front of his shirt and shoved hard.

"You cheated me!" Slocum shouted. "You are trying to do me out of my pay!"

"Not so, you surly barbarian. I paid you well for your services. It was not in our contract that you simply run off as you did. I assume you were out getting liquored up."

"You son of a bitch!" Slocum kicked back his chair and went for his Colt. At the same time Samuel Benbow lashed out, kicking Slocum hard in the gut. Slocum gasped and dropped to one knee. Benbow scattered the breakfast dishes all over as he swept them away with his arm. His fist ended its quick journey at the tip of Slocum's chin.

Slocum got his six-shooter out and fired a shot, but it

went wild. Plaster exploded in the wall and showered down on them. Benbow stepped up and kicked Slocum hard in the arm. He dropped his six-gun and rolled to protect himself from further kicks.

But they never came. Slocum groaned and tried to get to his feet and slipped back, blocking the way of Hunter and the other deputies with him.

"You let him get away, Slocum," Hunter accused.

"Quiet," grated Slocum, rubbing his arm. He picked up his six-shooter and stuffed it back in the holster. "I was trying to establish an alibi for why I killed him. I figured I could gun them both down, making it look like an accident that his wife got in the way."

"Smart thinking," grumbled Buck Stinson, "except you let both of them get clean away."

Slocum shoved past Stinson and went into the small kitchen at the rear of the café.

"Where'd they go?" he demanded of the cook. The man pointed at the back door and then shrugged his shoulders, as if saying he didn't know more than that. Slocum rushed out the back, drawing his six-shooter as he ran. Bursting into the bright Montana sun, he looked up and down the alley for any sign of the Benbows. They had vanished into thin air.

"They are running and will try to hightail it out of town," said Buck Stinson, coming around the side of the café. "We'll do it for you, Slocum."

"There's no need," Slocum said coldly. "Plummer wanted me to kill them and I will." Slocum turned toward the outskirts of town and said, "They won't be heading in that direction. Not on foot." He spun and stalked off in the other direction, heading toward the livery.

As he neared the stable, a bullet sang through the air and knocked off his Stetson. Slocum ducked and rolled behind a watering tank. He came to his knees, six-gun in hand. He looked for some sign of Samuel Benbow and saw nothing.

"He's trying to ambush you, Slocum," crowed Stinson, amused at the prospect. "You shoulda killed him when you had a chance. Looks like you're gonna get ventilated."

"Stay here and see who gets a bullet put in his belly," Slocum said. He poked his head up fast, ducked, and drew another round. He got to his feet and sprinted for a stack of hay. Benbow fired twice more. Slocum looked back and saw Stinson trying to strike a lucifer. The deputy intended to burn the stable to the ground.

"Don't!" shouted Slocum. "You'll take the entire town with you." Slocum waved and got Bill Hunter's attention from down the street. The second deputy came at a run.

"Stop that jackass before he gets us all killed," Slocum said, pointing at Stinson. Again Hunter and Stinson exchanged hot words. Slocum waited until the argument died and Stinson withdrew a few paces, arms crossed angrily over his chest.

When he was sure the deputies watched him closely, Slocum moved from behind the haystack and drew more fire from inside the stable. The slug came close, but Slocum kept running. He slammed hard into the side of the barn and pressed his back against it. Instinct told him to drop to the ground. An instant after he did, three more shots ripped through the wooden wall, sending splinters flying outward. If he had stayed where he had been, he would have been buzzard bait.

Crawling fast, Slocum got to the side and pried up a board that had come loose. He wiggled through and into the barn.

"You make killing you damned hard, Benbow," Slocum shouted. "Give it up. Nothing'll happen to you if you surrender."

"Like hell, Slocum!" came the angry cry, followed by two more slugs.

He heard Benbow reloading his small rimfire pistol. Slocum waited a moment, then edged toward the main doors.

He kicked one open, ducked, and let a slug whine past his head. The round sent water spraying upward from the watering tank. Two more rounds drove Plummer's deputies for cover.

"We can keep gnawing away at each other," Slocum said, "or we can go out in the street and finish this like men."

"You damned barbarian!"

"What'll it be, Benbow?"

"A real gunfight in the street? Just the pair of us?"

"Right now. In the main street. The law won't interfere."

"You deserve to be shot down like a rabid dog," Benbow shouted. Then in a quieter voice, said, "All right. To the street, Slocum. Just the two of us, *mano a mano*."

Backing away, Slocum got into the yard in front of the livery. He slowly replaced his Colt Navy in its holster and stood with his feet widespread.

Tension rippled along his shoulders as he waited for Benbow to appear. Then he saw the man come from the shadows of the livery. He had his Smith & Wesson tucked into his belt where he could go for it when the time was right.

"Now, Benbow, draw now!" shouted Slocum.

Benbow went for his small pistol just as Slocum grabbed his heavier Colt. Never had Slocum moved faster or shot more accurately. Samuel Benbow jerked upright, a surprised expression on his face.

"I'm dead," he said in a choked voice, then fell facedown in the dust. From all directions came Plummer's deputies. Hunter clapped Slocum on the back and Stinson looked as if he had eaten a sour apple. The other lawmen walked forward to examine Benbow.

One rolled him over. Blood had spread across the man's chest.

"Never seen a galoot bleed so much from a single shot," muttered one.

"It's all that hot air inside leakin' out," another said.

"Get him over to the undertaker's," Slocum said. "I might have killed him, but I owe him something more than a grave out in the potter's field. Who runs the best funeral parlor?"

"To hell with the best," grumbled Stinson. "Take him to the nearest. That's Old Man Garston's across the street."

Slocum followed as two of the deputies carried Benbow's body, one hanging onto his arms and the other holding his legs.

"We ought to be able to strip off them fancy-ass boots of his," one deputy said. "He won't need 'em where he's going."

"Show some respect for the dead," Slocum said in a menacing voice. "I shot him and I get to say how he's buried. He'll go into his grave wearing all those crazy duds."

"You don't have to get mad, Slocum," muttered the deputy who had coveted Benbow's boots.

The two men dropped Benbow onto the floor of the funeral parlor. Isaac Garston bustled from the back room and peered over the rims of his wire-frame glasses at the corpse.

"Oh, my, another unfortunate. Who might this be?" Garston peered closer, then straightened. "Why, this is that Englishman who was poking about asking all the questions. How did he meet his maker?"

"He got me riled," Slocum said. "He tried to cheat me and we shot it out."

"Well, yes, death by misadventure?" Isaac Garston looked around the ring of deputies, waiting for one of them to dispute Slocum's claim. When none did, the undertaker rubbed his hands together and said, "Who'll be taking care of the funeral expenses?"

"I will. It's the least I can do—and I mean the least," Slocum said. He peeled off a few bills from the roll Benbow had given him as pay for his services. "See that he gets a pine box and a planting before sundown tonight.''

''Very well. No need to let the flies at him, now is there?'' Garston clapped his hands and two young boys, possibly his sons, hurried from the back and hoisted Benbow up.

''One down, one to go,'' Slocum said. ''I don't cotton much to killing women.''

''Yeah, we found that out,'' Stinson said. ''What makes Gloria Benbow any different?''

''This time I was told to shoot her,'' Slocum said. ''And I was told by the *boss*.'' He emphasized the last word to put Buck Stinson in his place. The deputy started to take a swing at Slocum, but the others held him back. One whispered furiously in the deputy's ear until he settled down.

''I don't know what your game is, Slocum, but when I find out it'll be you and me. And I'm not some squirrely Englishman who hardly knows which end of the gun to hold.''

''Any time, Buck,'' Slocum said, pushing past the deputy. Slocum stepped onto Bannack's main street and began his search for Gloria Benbow. All day he hunted. Henry Plummer sent more and more deputies to join the hunt but by sundown, when Isaac Garston drove the small wagon bearing the pine box with Benbow's body in to the cemetery, Gloria Benbow had not been found.

Slocum stood silently and watched as the undertaker lowered the box into the shallow grave. He turned and almost bumped into the sheriff.

''I'll keep looking for her,'' Slocum said.

''No need, Slocum,'' Plummer replied. ''I've had all my boys hunting the live-long day and they haven't unearthed her.'' He laughed as he stared past Slocum at the boys shoveling dirt onto Benbow's coffin.

''Sooner or later, she will turn up,'' Slocum said.

''I'm sure she will, Slocum,'' answered Plummer.

"When she does, you'll have the honor and duty of killing her too. Until then, we're going back to camp."

This time Slocum rode to Road Agent Rock without a blindfold.

15

Slocum grew increasingly uneasy as he watched Henry Plummer with his two lieutenants. Both Buck Stinson and Bill Hunter seemed to glance in Slocum's direction more than they should. Slocum had figured he would be accepted unconditionally into the gang after they saw Samuel Benbow planted six feet in the ground. It hadn't worked that way. If anything, Plummer had grown more cautious around Slocum, even to the point of abruptly stopping a conversation with others when Slocum came close.

"What do you figure, Slocum?" asked an outlaw. The tall, scrawny man called Rails picked at his blackened teeth with the tip of a bowie knife. "Figure we will have another robbery soon?"

"Never cared much for garrison duty," Slocum said. He wished he had paid more attention to the courier's packet and the date Gloria had forged. The first robbery had been real. The dead guard and shotgun messenger on the stagecoach attested to that. Would the next gold shipment be real or a trap with federal marshals waiting?

"Reckon that's what this is, though I never thought of it that way. I was with the cavalry for a spell," Rails said in his slow drawl. "Didn't cotton much to it, so I lit out one night when I was supposed to be on guard duty."

"So the Army is looking for you?"

Rails shrugged. "Can't say that they are. Can't say they've even missed me much. I wasn't too good a soldier. This is the life for me. Laying around without much to do, then a spell of excitement and some money to spend when it's all said and done."

"Not much money from each robbery," Slocum said, sowing the seeds of discord whenever he could. "We ought to split it up evenly after every robbery. The ones of us that take the most risk ought to be getting the most gold."

Rails thought on this a while, spat, then finally said, "I thought like that when I first signed on, but I came to believe the boss's way is better."

"He keeps the lion's share while we get shot up for nothing more than worthless local bank scrip?"

"Naw, Slocum, it's not like that at all." Rails spat again and then tucked the knife into his boot top. "We get enough money from every job to get by. Nothing too extravagant, but enough to keep us in whiskey and ante for a hand of poker. The rest is put into a big pile. At the end of the year when we split up, everyone gets an even share then. So I'm getting pieces of all the others' robberies without having to risk my neck for it."

"But they are getting a piece of yours," Slocum insisted. "What if the robberies you do are the biggest? You take the biggest risk, you ought to get the biggest piece of the pie."

"This works just fine for me. If they get themselves

killed along the way, that makes my slice all the bigger.''

Slocum had the uneasy feeling that more—lots more— of Plummer's gang would be killed as the end of the ''hunting'' season neared. And it wouldn't be the guards on the gold shipments doing the killing. The gang members would be shooting one another in the back to increase their share of the big haul.

Slocum had to hand it to Plummer. The man had created a perfect scheme for robbery. The outlaws accepted only a small portion of the gold every time, thinking they would be rich in less than a year. Such naive trust hardly seemed normal among such road agents, though. Why should they trust Henry Plummer to give them anything?

Sure that none of them suspected Plummer of killing them off a few at a time until he finally had only a handful to deal with, Slocum decided not to push the matter any further. If he couldn't plant the seeds of discontent, there was no reason to come right out and tell Rails and the others what their fate would be.

Slocum smiled wryly. Hell, Henry Plummer might even arrest the lot of them and turn them over to the law in other parts of the country for the rewards. Rails would be tried as a deserter and put in front of a firing squad if the cavalry ever caught up with him. A standing reward of one hundred dollars rode on every deserter's head. Slocum didn't doubt the others in Plummer's gang had similar tales to tell.

Who better than a sheriff to know exactly what rewards were offered for each of the owlhoots riding to steal still another gold shipment?

Slocum lounged back as he watched Plummer and his two men talking in guarded tones. From time to time they cast a quick glance in his direction, as if to be sure he hadn't run off. The idea had struck Slocum as a good one time and again, but they watched him too closely to make it happen easily.

Besides, Slocum wasn't quite sure where Plummer's

treasure trove lay. He knew the particular trail leading to
it, but had no clue how the sheriff secured his gold. Henry
Plummer was too cautious a man to simply throw the bags
of gold dust and heavy bars of the precious metal out on
the ground in plain sight.

Slocum sat up when the trio of outlaws walked toward
him. He turned slightly so his Colt Navy was easy at hand
if needed. From the storm clouds perpetually on Buck Stinson's face, Slocum read nothing. But Bill Hunter looked
worried—and Plummer looked foxy.

That worried Slocum more than anything else.

"Slocum," called the sheriff. "We got another robbery
to do. A heavy freight wagon is rattling along from Nevada
City on its way south."

"How much gold and how many guards and when do
we go?" Slocum asked.

"I appreciate a man who is eager to become rich but not
so eager he will endanger himself and his partners," Plummer said carefully. The way the sheriff talked put Slocum
on guard even more.

Slocum got to his feet. Stinson backed off, hand moving
in the direction of his six-gun. Ignoring him, Slocum faced
Plummer.

"Who all is going?"

"You, Rails, maybe Callahan, Adobe Jack, and Marcus."

Slocum took a deep breath to settle his thundering heart.
The men Plummer named were all ones Slocum counted as
expendable. Losing them would only increase the take for
the remaining outlaws and not make anyone the least bit
uncomfortable.

"Is Stinson leading the robbery? Or is Hunter?" Slocum
probed for more information. Plummer was holding back.
What he got convinced him something was seriously
wrong.

"Why, Slocum, we are so pleased with the way you

removed Samuel Benbow from our trail, we decided to let you take the lead this time. Show us your best. Make us all smile when you come riding back with the gold bars gleaming.'' Henry Plummer smiled insincerely, looking more like a grinning sidewinder than a man.

"I'll do my best," Slocum said, wondering if this was his best chance for simply riding on and leaving Road Agent Rock behind. Somehow, he doubted it from the way Stinson and Hunter eyed him. There would be spies all along the way to the robbery to make sure he didn't simply ride off—and there might be even more if he was successful in stealing the gold.

"Here's a map of the location for the robbery. Get there by sundown and you can catch the freighter thinking they are safe. Ride straight on back to camp."

Slocum turned the map over and studied it. He wished for the hundredth time he could remember which of the robberies Gloria had altered. She had distracted him too much, he realized, and now he might pay for that with his life.

Slocum tucked the map into his pocket. His eyes met Henry Plummer's for a moment. The sheriff's poker expression betrayed not a flicker of emotion.

Slocum spun and hurried off to round up the men going with him without another word to either the sheriff or his deputies. To the others in the gang he had proven himself by gunning down Samuel Benbow when ordered to do so. Not finding Gloria Benbow wasn't really his fault. All of Plummer's deputies had scoured Bannack for her and had been unable to find her. The gossip in camp was that she had started running and wouldn't stop until she reached the shores of Merry Olde England.

Slocum settled his saddle, got the cinch tight, then kneed the horse in the belly to make her expel the air she had been holding. As the belly relaxed, Slocum cinched down even tighter. He wasn't going to be tossed off his horse like a greenhorn. Riding as hard as he could might be necessary to save his hide.

As the small group trotted away from the huge red monolith, Slocum noted that Buck Stinson and a half dozen others were saddling too. Were they ordered to follow him? Or did Plummer have more than one robbery going on this afternoon? Slocum wished he knew.

Making his way through the maze of canyons proved easier every time Slocum rode. The small group emerged along the Alder Gulch Road an hour before sundown, perfect timing for getting the lay of the land and finding the best spot to waylay the wagon carrying hundreds of pounds of freshly poured gold bars.

"You want to catch 'em in a cross fire?" asked Rails. "That's about my favorite method of stopping 'em in their tracks. They look one way, see guns. They look the other, thinking to run, and see guns. 'Bout then they give it up."

"A good plan," Slocum agreed. If he had planned the robbery himself, he would have had scouts far down the road to report on the wagon's approach. He needed to know how many guards were on the freighter and how difficult it would be to get away with the gold after stealing it. They might need to keep the wagon and leave the driver and guards on foot—or dead.

Slocum turned and stared at the trail behind. He had the feeling of being watched.

"Jack!" Slocum called. "Adobe Jack! Backtrack a ways and see if anyone is following us. Don't try to find out anything about them. Just let me know if you see anyone."

"Why you sendin' Jack?" asked Rails. "He's not that good a tracker." Rails spat. "Fact is, Adobe Jack's not too bright."

That was exactly why Slocum had sent him. If he reported back he had found no one, that didn't mean they weren't being followed by Stinson and others from the gang. But Jack would never be able to lie if he did see anyone. That was the sole reason Slocum had chosen him for the backtracking.

"Keeps him occupied while we set up for the robbery," Slocum lied.

"You want me to scout down the road to see if I can spot the wagon?"

"Send Marcus. He hasn't done much to earn his keep," Slocum said. Rails was hardly a friend but he was friendly. That made Slocum want to keep him by his side, at least until the robbery started. Then it might be time to simply hightail it.

But that mountain of gold Henry Plummer had put away still drew Slocum powerfully. It was riches for the taking and the only people who would miss it had already counted it as lost a long time back.

He might not even get shot at if he could find the hoard and had a chance to load some of it on a pack mule or two.

"Marcus," Rails said, lifting his chin and indicating the man riding hard to get back to them. "Either he's got a burr under his saddle or he spotted the wagon."

Slocum nodded. He craned his neck to see if Adobe Jack had spotted Stinson or any of the others behind them. It made sense to Slocum that they would let him steal the gold, taking all the bullets, then have Buck Stinson and the others he had seen riding out with the deputy come swooping down to take it away.

Slocum didn't doubt he would join Rails and the others knocking at the Pearly Gates in a very short time when Stinson showed. *If* Stinson did. Plummer played a complicated game, and Slocum wasn't sure he understood everything about how the sheriff operated.

"Check your six-shooters," Slocum ordered. "We've got a robbery to perform."

Adobe Jack came riding up. Slocum glanced at him. The man smiled and shook his head. Nothing on their trail.

"Let's get ready, gents," Slocum said, pulling his bandanna up to mask his face. The wagon clattered into view and came even with them. Slocum looked left and right, then gave the signal. Rails and Jack fired into the air to draw attention to the robbery. Then they rode down the slope toward the wagon. Slocum turned wary when he saw the driver's reaction.

The man showed no sign of being afraid. Without a shotgun messenger riding alongside him in the box, he ought to have been pissing his pants.

"Wait," Slocum called, but he was too late. The tarp covering the rear of the wagon fluttered in the breeze, then was thrown back to reveal a half-dozen men, all armed with rifles or shotguns.

"Throw down your guns!" one man in the wagon bed shouted. But the words had hardly left his lips when the others opened fire.

Slocum watched in horror as Rails snapped upright in the saddle, then tumbled off his horse. Slocum knew the scrawny man was dead before he hit the ground. A slug whined by his own ear and forced him to duck. From behind him Adobe Jack let out a whoop and charged.

"Don't do it, Jack," Slocum begged, but it did no good. Jack had fixed only one thing in his brain and intended to carry it out. He wanted to rescue Rails.

He died, just as his friend had. And then the gunfight started in earnest. Marcus had jumped off his mount and taken shelter behind a large rock. He used his rifle to pick off first one, then another of the men in the wagon. Slocum saw the gleam of light off more than one federal marshal's badge in that wagon.

He had wondered if this might be the fake shipment, the one Gloria had engineered with her forgery. Slocum knew he had no time to decide if it was or if the marshals had finally had enough of Plummer's gang and their depredations and had laid this trap all by themselves.

Another round almost took Slocum out of the saddle. Hot

pain lanced through his arm and a sluggish flow turned his arm sticky. Rather than return fire, Slocum edged his horse around and started out down the road at a dead gallop.

Marcus let out a cry from behind. Slocum didn't have to look to know the man had also died. The only one returning fire now was Callahan. Shotguns roared, and then only silence reigned along the Alder Gulch Road. Slocum kept riding hard, knowing he could never explain his way out of this if the Helena marshal arrested him.

And he sure as hell would never be able to explain what went wrong to Henry Plummer. The Bannack sheriff would believe the worst because he had never trusted Slocum in the first place, even after Slocum had seen Samuel Benbow put under the dirt in the cemetery.

Just as Slocum thought he was away scot-free, a single shot rang out. He felt his horse stumble, recover, and keep running. But the horse weakened swiftly, forcing Slocum to rein back. He dropped to the ground and ran his hand along the horse's shoulder. The bullet had caught the horse high on the flank. Even as he pressed his hand into the horse's flesh, she weakened.

Seconds later, the horse shuddered and keeled over. She gave a final kick after hitting the ground before she died. Slocum stared at the dead animal, then knew he had to hightail it. But his rifle was pinned under the deadweight of the horse's body. Rather than waste time, Slocum started to lose himself in the tumble of rocks along the road.

He hadn't taken a dozen steps when he discovered the source of the slug that had ripped the life from his horse. He stared up at a federal deputy with a rifle aimed directly at him.

Slocum looked left and right, hunting for a place to make his stand against the lawman. The neighing of horses and the rattle of a wagon in the road spun him around. The wagon laden with the ambushing marshals was only a few yards away. And the riders approaching from the other direction were also lawmen.

Slocum slowly raised his hands. To put up any fight now meant his immediate death—not that it mattered too much. As a road agent he was likely to be strung up on the spot, if they could find a tree tall enough.

16

Slocum spun about, then slowly lowered his six-gun and put his hands up. He was no fool. If he so much as looked cross-eyed at the lawmen, they would fill him full of holes. They might also string him up, but Slocum knew he would gain a few minutes by not trying to fight his way out of a ring of certain death.

As he turned around slowly, he counted no fewer than eight federal deputies. He tried to pick out the marshal in charge, but could not.

"You got me," Slocum said, keeping his hands high. "I can explain what's going on."

"It's plain as the nose on your face what you were up to, you low-down, bushwhackin' road agent!"

Slocum closed his eyes for a moment, imagining a bullet ripping through him. None came.

"I think we caught ourselves the gang's leader," said another voice. Slocum tried to place it. Although it was familiar, he wasn't able to put a name to it.

Slocum's mind had turned to how best to escape when he heard the steady crunch of boots on rock and gravel behind him. He glanced over his shoulder, hoping for any opportunity to get away. His jaw dropped when he saw who was there.

"Yep, that's God's truth. This here just might be the gang leader," said Samuel Benbow, smiling broadly. "Then again, it might be the gent I told you about who is helping us get the goods on Henry Plummer."

"Benbow!" Slocum felt a flood of relief. "Tell them I'm not—"

"Is he really in cahoots with you—with us?" asked a deputy.

"He is indeed, my good man," said Benbow, his words and tone again that of the fictitious Lord Benbow. "Mr. Slocum's aid has been invaluable in helping get all the evidence we need on Plummer and his cronies."

Slocum heaved a sigh of relief as the circle of leveled rifles slowly faded. One by one the deputies dropped their aim and moved on to find other targets.

"I was beginning to think I actually planted you in the cemetery," Slocum said. "You're looking mighty fine for a corpse."

"Never felt better. The ambush went according to plan." Benbow stretched and rubbed his belly where it had appeared Slocum had shot him. "The chicken blood I smeared all over myself was the devil's own work getting off. Ruined my shirt."

"The undertaker didn't try robbing Gloria, did he?" asked Slocum.

"An undertaker who isn't a thief? Come, come, John. You ought to know better than that. He wanted two hundred dollars to certify my death and to carry out the fake burial. He even tried to make the funeral expenses additional, until I pointed out he could dig up the pine box later and reuse it.''

"He would have anyway," said Slocum. He and Benbow walked down the slope to the road. The wagon laden with federal deputies rumbled along and stopped close by.

"All I wanted was to make Plummer think I was dead and that you had carried out his orders. It must have worked. Here you are." In a lower voice Benbow added, "And it seemed that you were in charge of the robbery."

Slocum frowned. "Plummer is playing a complicated game. He did not trust me. I think he suspected a trap."

"Ah, he wanted you killed. You and the other poor fools who tried to shoot it out with half of all the federal lawmen in the territory. Or perhaps he knew this was a fake shipment and wanted to see what happened. If you came back with gold but no road agents behind you, he would know you were working for the law."

"Where did Gloria vanish to back in Bannack? All of Plummer's men hunted for her but couldn't find hide nor hair."

"I'll let her tell you all about it later." Benbow jumped into the wagon bed and sat, his legs swinging back and forth. He obviously thought hard about something. Slocum knew what it was.

"There's still nothing to tie Plummer to your father's death," Slocum said. "Even if he had ridden out with me on this job, the worst that might have happened is that he would be tried for robbery."

"He is a careful man, that Henry Plummer," agreed Benbow. "I have long since realized he will never be held accountable for my father's death—not in any court of law." Benbow fingered the six-shooter holstered at his side. "There are other kinds of justice, higher laws."

"Would him being sent to prison be good enough?" Slocum asked. He knew the answer. If a lawman had killed his father, he would never have rested until the man was also very, very dead.

The hot glare he got from Samuel Benbow told him the answer.

"Hey, Benbow," came a shout from down the road. A heavyset man with a bushy handlebar mustache rode up. His badge was a little bigger, a little gaudier, than the deputies'. Slocum knew he was looking at the federal marshal.

"Marshal Kline, did you round them all up?" asked Benbow.

"Got the lot of them. All are dead,'ceptin' this one, and you tole my deputies he's the one who set up the ambush."

"He is," Benbow agreed. "Was there any trace of Henry Plummer?"

"Not a shred of proof he's behind this gang," Kline said, twirling his mustache nervously. "Them's serious charges you're makin' 'gainst a duly elected sheriff. I think we got the varmints what been robbin' up and down Alder Gulch."

"That's the easy answer," Slocum said. "There are thirty more waiting at Road Agent Rock."

"Road Agent Rock? What the hell's that?" The marshal shifted in the saddle, as if he had worn sores on his butt in the ride down from Helena.

"That's where the outlaws camp out, Marshal. I told you about it, as reported by Mr. Slocum here." Benbow exchanged a quick look with Slocum. They both knew the day's hunt for road agents was over. Marshal Kline wanted nothing more than to go home in triumph, having shot up the gang of highwaymen that had been plaguing freighters and miners along the Alder Gulch Road.

"You boys find me more proof, especially about that snake Plummer. I've had my heart set on runnin' him out of the territory for quite a while. Never did cotton much to him or his citified ways."

The wagon rattled along, stopping at the site of the robbery. The deputies loaded the bodies into the back of the wagon.

"Much obliged to you for lettin' us in on your party," Marshal Kline said. "You want a ride back to Helena?"

"I will return with you," Benbow said, keeping Slocum from answering by a hand on his shoulder. "Leave Mr. Slocum here to tend my camp." In a lower voice Benbow said, "I'll get the horses and come back for you both."

"Gloria's in your camp?"

Benbow laughed and waved as the wagon lurched and started toward distant Helena. For a few minutes Slocum stood in the center of the rutted dirt road, wondering where Benbow's camp might be. Then he decided it wasn't going to come to him. He had to go to it.

Studying the side of the road, he found hoofprints from two horses. Following them into the hills led him to a small, protected area in the foothills. His nose wrinkled when he caught a hint of stew cooking. His belly grumbled. Slocum couldn't remember the last time he had eaten, and the odor of anything more than beans was bound to make his mouth water.

"I wondered when you'd show up, John," said Gloria teasingly. Slocum spun, hand flashing to his Colt Navy. He relaxed when he saw her sprawled on a rock in the growing darkness after sundown.

"It's mighty risky spooking me like that," he told her. He settled his six-shooter back into the holster and slipped the leather thong keeper back over the hammer. Slocum didn't need this kind of firepower right now.

"Fixed some victuals," Gloria said, sliding off the rock. Slocum moved fast and caught her before she landed. The sultry, dark-haired woman made quite an armful.

Their faces were only inches apart. Slocum bent a little and kissed her. She returned the kiss with ardor, then lithely twisted and jumped from his arms.

"Tell me all about the robbery," she said, her breath

coming faster. Slocum watched the rise and fall of her ample breasts and fought to keep his mind on what she was asking.

"Plummer is a sharp character," Slocum said. "I don't think he ever trusted me, even after we faked your brother's death back in Bannack." The words "your brother" rolled off Slocum's tongue like honey now. Gloria Benbow was not married. This put things right with Slocum and his upbringing.

"Are you saying he wasn't caught?" Her blue eyes widened, then narrowed as a set came to her jaw. Slocum had seen determination before, but never like this. Gloria Benbow was one determined woman, and he was glad he wasn't standing between her and her goal of seeing Henry Plummer swing.

"The others with me were all the dregs of the gang," Slocum said. "Ones Plummer—or Hunter and Stinson— wanted to be rid of." Slocum didn't bother explaining the method of paying off the outlaws, that the fewer in the gang at the end of the year, the more Plummer and his cronies kept.

"So we still have to cut the head off this monster calling himself a lawman," Gloria said between clenched teeth.

Slocum helped himself to the stew cooking on the campfire as Gloria muttered to herself about all that she wanted to do to Henry Plummer. Again, Slocum was glad he didn't wear a badge in Bannack. The spitfire's vengeance was not likely to be limited only to the sheriff.

Satisfied with the meal, Slocum leaned back and watched Gloria for a moment. Their eyes locked. She was flushed from her rage at having again failed to catch Henry Plummer. Slocum rose and went to her.

Without saying a word, he sank down beside her bedroll and took her in his arms.

"John, no, not now. I don't feel like it."

He kissed her. The power and anger flooded forth and

filled him with energy. And as he continued to kiss her that energy flowed back, filling her, building Gloria into a passionate paramour. She melted into his embrace as her anger turned to ardor.

Slocum's kisses left her lips and slipped down to her neck. Gloria threw her head back and let him work even lower, between her breasts. With his tongue he worked the buttons free, then found fleshy ones capping each of her succulent mounds of flesh. The nipples had hardened into coppery points that he sucked into his mouth. Gentle nibbling caused her to arch her back and moan with every stroke of his tongue.

"You excite me, John. Don't stop. Don't you dare stop!"

That was the farthest thing from his mind. He worked her free of her blouse and tugged at her skirt. It took both of them to get it off. Gloria hurried to escape the confines of her frilly undergarments. As she worked, so did Slocum. He shucked off his gun belt and stripped off shirt and boots. Gloria helped him get out of his pants, her hands stroking here and there as he wiggled.

"You are going to get a chill," she joked, her hand curled around his hardened shaft. Stroking gently, she coaxed him to a steely hardness that quivered in the circle of her fingers.

"Don't expect to leave it out in the air that long," he said. His own hands worked down the woman's sleek sides to the soft furry triangle between her thighs. He gently parted her legs and opened the gates of paradise.

Gloria gasped as his finger entered and worked around inside. She lay back, her thighs opening willingly to him.

"You're right, John, as you always are. I don't think you'll be out in the air long at all."

"Long enough," he said, positioning himself. Slocum looked down into her lust-fogged eyes and tried to remember ever having found a more desirable woman. He couldn't. Gloria was smart, beautiful—and deadly. He had to keep telling himself that she would pull the trigger and never think twice about it if she had the chance to kill Henry Plummer.

"Don't torment me," she pleaded. "I need you so much!"

His hands cupped her buttocks and stroked over the fleshy half-moons as he positioned their bodies. Then Slocum slid forward. The tip of his manhood penetrated dewy nether lips and surged deep into her interior. It felt as if she gripped him with a velvet glove. Then Gloria used hidden muscles to clamp down hard on his manhood.

It was Slocum's turn to gasp with pleasure. Pulling back slowly, he withdrew until only the empurpled tip remained within her. Then he plunged forward again and found paradise.

Gloria managed to sit up and clasp her arms around his neck. She kissed him repeatedly. Slocum found it impossible to keep moving in and out. He fell back, sitting on his knees. Gloria swarmed up and positioned herself with her legs on either side of his body. Lowering quickly, she again took him deeply into her moist interior.

"Don't stop, John," Gloria begged.

"Hard to move like this," he said, but even as he spoke, he reached around, cupped her buttocks, and lifted. Rising and then falling, her body seemed to surround him totally. Her breasts rubbed against his chest and he felt her hot breath coming faster and faster. Most of all, the intense pressures mounting in his loins were not to be denied.

He moved faster and parted her firm ass cheeks, only to crush them together. This tightened her around him even more. Gloria tossed her head back like a frisky filly and shrieked out her joy as orgasm crashed through her. Release of Slocum's tensions followed seconds later. Falling forward, Slocum pinned her to the ground. His hips moved of their own accord until he was entirely spent.

"John, I feel so drained," Gloria said. "But I also feel so . . . filled with vigor." She snuggled closer. The sweat from their bodies turned them slick, but Slocum didn't mind.

"We're going to get a chill if we don't get dressed," Gloria said, ever practical.

"There's no hurry. Your brother said he was going to get more horses before he comes back. But he didn't say why."

"The three of us are going to head into the canyons and root out Henry Plummer, that's why. It was part of our plan. If we didn't catch him red-handed at the robbery, then we agreed to ride to this Road Agent Rock you keep mentioning."

"We?"

"You have to lead us in, John. You're the only one who really knows the countryside well enough."

"Plummer has more than thirty men with him. There's no way three of us could stand a snowball's chance in Hell of getting in and out of there alive."

"You are so negative about these things, John," Gloria chided. "We can do it. We have to. I have the feeling Plummer is nearing the end of his raiding. If he gets enough gold, he might move on and we will never bring him to justice."

Mention of Plummer's stash caused Slocum to think hard. Going back to Road Agent Rock wasn't too bright, but maybe they could sneak in and find the gold. It would be enough to make them all rich.

Slocum glanced at Gloria, and knew then that being rich wasn't what she was after. Her eyes fixed on him and she read the indecision. The blouse she had been putting on came open, revealing the creamy cones of her breasts. Slocum damned himself for thinking with his balls rather than his head, then succumbed.

He and Gloria had finished making love again just minutes before her brother rode into the small camp trailing three horses.

17

"Not interrupting anything, am I?" called Samuel Benbow. The man laughed as he slid his leg over the battered pommel and dropped to the ground. Slocum hitched his pants and settled his cross-draw holster so it didn't look as if he had just fastened it. It bothered Slocum a mite that Gloria's brother didn't seem to much mind what had been going on. A man ought to be willing to protect a wife's—or sister's—honor.

"Gloria and I have been discussing what's next," Slocum said. He glanced over his shoulder at Gloria. She looked positively beautiful and not a little wicked. She licked her red lips, the tip of her tongue slowly working around in seductive invitation to him. He realized that once again he was thinking with his balls, not with his head.

And he knew better than to let greed drive him. Yet only

a distant part of his brain screamed out that it was purely and simply dumb to ride back into the canyons protecting Henry Plummer and his gang.

Slocum closed his eyes for a moment, and was deluged with pictures of a mound of gold stolen over the years by Plummer, mixed with enticing glimpses of Gloria smiling up at him—and over it all was the red monolith that dominated Plummer's camp.

Road Agent Rock.

He cursed himself as a completely greedy, love-besotted fool. He knew what drove Gloria and her brother. They wanted Plummer brought to justice for killing their father, and even thought it was still possible to bring the wily sheriff to trial. Slocum doubted that. The sheriff had shown himself to be a careful schemer, willing to sacrifice all his men to stay free. And to get richer.

How long would it be until Gloria and Samuel Benbow decided Plummer would never be arrested by the Helena marshal and had to be killed for his crimes?

Slocum was no hired killer, but he found his hand twitching involuntarily at the idea of reaching for the ebony handle of his six-shooter and sending a round into Plummer's chest. Too many times the sheriff had tried to put Slocum into a grave. Slocum would not give the road agent another chance.

"I got the horses a sight quicker than I thought," Benbow said, twisting the reins into a braid and putting a heavy rock on top of the bundle. "If you and Gloria have been talking it over, then all that remains is to ask which way we ride."

"John doesn't want to go back, do you, John." Gloria's tone was a mixture of banter and accusation. With it came a hint of promise. Slocum wasn't stupid. He knew what the lovely woman pledged in return for his cooperation.

"You'll be riding into the mouth of a grizzly," Slocum warned.

"We've been living within spitting distance of that big old bear," Gloria said.

"Slocum, we haven't entered into this enterprise blindly," Benbow said. "We know Plummer is a dangerous man, more so than you." Benbow's jaw tensed, and a hardness came to his eyes that Slocum had witnessed only in passing before. This was no fop. Slocum had to remind himself that Samuel Benbow had played a role as surely as any actor in a melodeon. He was a man intent on revenge and not a British lord come to the West for a lark.

"Don't know why I'm getting involved," Slocum said, waiting for Benbow's response. When it came, it convinced him to continue, no matter how perilous the road.

"Go, stay, we don't care, Slocum," Benbow said. "We'll find our way to Plummer's camp and get him."

"There are still thirty or more outlaws with him. Simply riding up and asking him to surrender won't work."

Benbow's hand pressed into his coat. Outlined there was the gun he had used so ably before. It proved to Slocum how dedicated Benbow was, as if he had not known before.

"Let's ride," Slocum said. "We can get to their camp before dawn, if we don't rest."

"He's getting worried," Slocum said, pulling Gloria back to cover. Plummer had posted sentries on the narrow path leading to Road Agent Rock.

In the darkness before dawn it had been difficult to see the guards patrolling the canyons, but luck had coupled with Slocum's skill to avoid them. If a warning had been raised, Slocum knew he and the Benbows would have faced three dozen rifles and shotguns and been dead before the sun poked above the rocky rim.

"We can sneak by," Benbow insisted.

Slocum shook his head. "Not now. If Plummer has another guard at the far end of this rocky draw, we'd be caught like rats in a trap if anything went wrong."

"We can't ride around. That might take days," Gloria protested.

"Never said anything about going around," Slocum said, tossing his Stetson aside. He fumbled around and found his thick-bladed knife. Making sure his six-shooter was handy, he started into the dark. A hand on his arm stopped him.

Gloria's blue eyes shone like moons in the night. She gave him a quick kiss and a smile that augured for the future. Then Gloria faded into shadow, disappearing from sight. He sighed, and then focused his attention on the lookout slowly pacing on a rocky ledge. Slocum fell flat on his belly and wiggled forward quieter than any sidewinder slithering across the desert sand. When he came within ten paces of the guard, Slocum stopped and watched, some sense telling him of trouble.

The lookout rested his rifle against a rock and worked to build himself a smoke. This was the perfect time for Slocum to strike, but he held back. And then he knew he had been right. From nowhere came a voice. "How about offerin' me one too?"

"You're always bummin' fixin's off me," complained the sentry Slocum could see. From deep gloom came a second sentry, one Slocum had not even suspected. The two worked on making their cigarettes, then stood and smoked them. Slocum's eyes fixed on the burning red coals, his mind racing.

He got to his feet and pressed his back against the face of the cliff. Slocum sidled along as the pair shared their smoke. Then he swung about. One guard's eyes went wide. Slocum drove his knife into the other's belly.

"Wha—?" was all the first guard could say before Slocum's hand clamped on the man's throat. Rather than grabbing for the six-shooter at his hip, the guard tried to pry Slocum's steely hand away. That ended his life. Slocum got the knife free of its gory berth in the other man, now dead, and slashed quickly. More blood exploded, flowing black in the night. Slocum stepped away and let the second dead sentry fall. His blood flowed for only a few seconds, proof that he had died quickly and his heart had stopped pumping.

Slocum quietly retraced his steps and found Gloria and her brother silently waiting. He appreciated their silence. Others might have been chattering nervously.

"John?" asked Gloria.

"The path's clear, maybe into camp. I might have taken out all the guards here." Slocum led the way into the narrow entryway opening into the valley where Road Agent Rock dominated the landscape. He jerked hard on his horse's reins, stopped, and studied the high walls on either side, then knew he had eliminated all the guards there. Plummer would have been furious learning his lookouts had stood together, but there was nothing the outlaw leader could do to his incompetent men that Slocum had not already done.

"Let's get him," Benbow said. Slocum reached out and grabbed the man by the shoulder.

"We've been this road before," Slocum said. "Prying Plummer loose from that camp isn't likely to happen—not in this life."

"He's right, Samuel," said Gloria. "Plummer will have Stinson and all the others surrounding him."

"And there's nothing tying him to the robberies," Slocum went on. "You need evidence. If we can find something linking Plummer to the gang that will convince a jury, you still have to arrest him."

"He'd go down shooting," Benbow said, rubbing his chin. "I want to see his face when the judge pronounces sentence, but watching him squirm as I pull the trigger might be just as good."

"Only if he knows who we are," said Gloria.

Slocum let them weave their fantasies of revenge. He knew simply capturing Henry Plummer would be hard. Getting him convicted in any court might be impossible. And Slocum considered himself a good judge of character. He had seen Plummer's like before, and Plummer would never back down one inch if Benbow happened to get the drop on him. Plummer would die where he stood and never give Samuel or Gloria Benbow the pleasure of knowing they had won.

"His office is in Bannack," Slocum said slowly. "If he is in camp, he's got to return to town eventually. And if he's not in camp, he'll come on out to check on his men. Plummer's not the kind to trust even Hunter or Stinson too far."

"That's it!" Gloria cried. "We ambush him on the way out of camp, when he's not surrounded by all his gang. What a wonderful idea, John!"

If he had been much closer, Slocum knew the lovely dark-haired woman would have kissed him. He glanced sideways at Samuel Benbow. The woman's brother seemed not to have heard anything said. He certainly did not see the way Gloria stared at Slocum.

"He comes and goes along a secret route," Benbow said after a spell. "I tried tracking him more than once. That's another reason we hired you, Slocum. You're a better tracker. Maybe you can match Plummer's skill."

Slocum remembered how Benbow had spotted a trail that had been hidden from him, and doubted he was any better a scout than Samuel Benbow. But he had a notion Plummer's secret trail to Road Agent Rock lay on the far side of the monolith, out where Slocum had lost the sheriff before.

Out near where Slocum thought Plummer's treasure trove was hidden.

"We can sneak around and see what we can see," Slocum allowed. He began growing increasingly uneasy about the two dead guards back in the narrow draw leading to the outlaw camp. Plummer wasn't the kind of leader to let his

sentries stay at their post so long they grew careless—
though these two had. When their relief showed up and
found the two dead, there'd be hell to pay. Slocum wanted
to be far enough away that the other road agents never
found him.

The trio trotted their horses along the rocky wall until
they found a grassy slope leading down into a thicket. Slocum galloped along, the others trailing behind. Then, with
its flanks lathered from the exertion, his horse balked at
going farther. With the cover afforded by the trees, Slocum
was willing to let the horse rest while he scouted on foot.

"John, wait," called Gloria when she saw him striking
out on foot.

"I'll be back. I need to know if Plummer is in camp.
Don't do anything foolish," he warned. Slocum didn't want
to return and find the pair of them prisoners.

"John, be careful," Gloria said. She blew him a kiss.
Slocum grinned, then headed off, wary of the rising sun
revealing him to a bleary-eyed sentry pacing the perimeter
of the outlaws' camp.

It took Slocum almost an hour to decide that Plummer
was not in camp. But from the snippets of early morning
talk he overheard, the sheriff was returning to camp soon.
A new shipment of gold would soon fall to the road agents.

Slipping back, Slocum hightailed it for the copse and
found Samuel and Gloria waiting for him.

"Plummer's not there," he said, watching their faces.
Gloria's face fell. Her brother's hardened. Slocum read resolve—and death. Samuel Benbow intended to track down
Henry Plummer and kill him rather than worry about gathering evidence that the renegade sheriff had killed their father. Slocum knew it was time to bring it all to a head.

"He's coming in before noon, or so the men say," Slocum declared.

"We can capture him then!" cried Gloria.

"Where would he come from? We don't know where

his secret path into the valley is,'' said Samuel Benbow. The man's face was a mask of confusion. He wanted Plummer brought before a jury of twelve, convicted, and hanged. He also wanted the pleasure of watching Plummer squirm before he plugged him.

Without knowing how the sheriff got into the outlaw camp, there was little chance either would occur.

''That way,'' Slocum said, pointing toward the far side of the valley where he had lost Plummer before. It took the better part of the morning to arrive at a spot above the trail where Slocum had followed Plummer out of the camp. This time he wouldn't let the sheriff get away—and there would be a mountain of stolen gold waiting for him.

The sun beat down directly on top of Slocum's Stetson by the time they found a secure spot to lay their ambush. Slocum was able to see far up the valley toward the red rock monolith, giving them plenty of time if any of the gang came riding their way. The only drawback was having a view of only a few yards into the maze of canyon trails where he had followed Plummer before. The sheriff had to come from Bannack along this path, but where the secret stash of gold and other plunder from the outlaw's yearlong rampage was hidden was still a mystery to Slocum.

''You seem nervous, John,'' Gloria said in a low voice. ''Does the prospect of facing Plummer frighten you?''

He shook his head once, his sharp green eyes working along the trail for any hint that a heavy load had been dragged off to a hiding place.

''You are so . . . distracted,'' Gloria went on. Her hand rested warmly on his arm, breaking what concentration he had.

''We got business with Plummer,'' Slocum said.

''What about us?'' she asked in a low, intimate voice.

''There's no 'us' until this is over,'' Slocum said. ''You have fire in your belly but it's nothing like *his*.'' Slocum pointed to the spot where Samuel Benbow lay flat, using a pair of field glasses to study every inch of the trail. Not an ant could crawl out there without him spotting it.

"He and Papa were always close," Gloria allowed. "I want Plummer brought to justice, but with Samuel . . ." She shook her head.

"It's more for him. I think I know," Slocum said, remembering how he had felt hearing of his own father's death. If any man had been responsible, Slocum knew he would have gone to the ends of the earth to avenge that murder.

"Slocum!" came Benbow's sharp cry, cutting off any reply from his sister. "Rider coming. It's Plummer!"

"Get ready," Slocum said. They had positioned themselves to catch Plummer in a cross fire. If the sheriff refused to surrender, he would have to fight his way past them to get the support of the road agents. The gunfire might bring the outlaws running, but it would take them a spell before they figured out what was going on. By then, Slocum hoped to have Plummer all trussed up.

He might even have learned where Plummer's hoard waited for the right man to carry it off.

"Hold your fire, Slocum," Benbow urged. "Let *me* shoot if it becomes necessary."

Slocum shook his head. He wasn't the one getting so all-fired keyed up he would shoot at anything that moved. Slocum drew his Colt Navy and cocked it, waiting in hiding just off the narrow trail. Plummer had to come around a pile of rock before he would see the trap.

The clop-clop of hooves slowed, then stopped entirely, showing the rider was becoming leery of the trail. Slocum tried to think of any reason the outlaw might suspect an ambush.

"What happened to him, John?"

Slocum put his finger to his lips, cautioning Gloria to silence. He didn't know what was going on, and that worried him. Plummer ought to have ridden smack into their guns and hadn't.

Swinging around, Slocum chanced a quick look down the trail. Plummer had ridden to one side of the narrow canyon and was hunting for something. A grin crossed Slocum's face. Plummer had to be checking his gold. It was time to act.

"Slocum, get down!" came Benbow's cry. "There's a deputy with him!"

How he missed the second rider, Slocum didn't know. Only Benbow's warning saved him from getting a bullet in the head. Slocum jerked to his left, his Colt rising and firing at the same instant. He winged the deputy, knocking him out of the saddle. But Henry Plummer was too far for a good shot with a six-shooter.

Benbow used his rifle, but Slocum knew the result the instant the man fired.

Samuel Benbow had missed.

A crack like thunder echoed along the narrow trail. From the corner of his eye Slocum saw Benbow snap erect, then twist slightly as he sank to the ground with a bullet in him. Slocum got off two shots, but the range was too great. Coming with a new slug aimed at him was a taunting laugh. Then Sheriff Plummer was galloping out of range. They had missed their target.

But Plummer had not missed his. Gloria Benbow knelt by her brother, sobbing. Samuel Benbow did not move.

18

"John, please, he needs help," Gloria Benbow sobbed. She cradled her brother's head in her lap. From the pale, pinched look to Samuel Benbow's face, Slocum knew the man didn't have long unless a sawbones fixed him up quick. He knelt, ripped open the man's shirt, and examined the wound.

"He's one lucky galoot," Slocum said. As he probed the wound, Benbow winced. There was still life—and fight— in him. The man's eyes flickered open and he fixed his gaze on Slocum.

"Did you get him?"

"Plummer?" Slocum shook his head, not sure if Benbow saw or if the lights were being blown out one by one in the man's brain.

"Then I can't die," Benbow said, as if that settled everything. "Get me to a doctor."

Slocum gnawed at his lower lip, thinking hard. Henry Plummer knew someone was gunning for him now. He might not know who, but he was suspicious and would immediately realize Slocum had not died in the abortive robbery if he caught sight of him. And if they rode into Bannack with a wounded Samuel Benbow, the sheriff would know he had been duped and kill the lot of them. After all, Benbow was supposed to be buried out in the town's cemetery.

From the look of the wound, he might end there yet.

"We can't stay here," Slocum said. The gunshots would draw the road agents like flies to a fresh mound of cow pie.

"If we move him, he'll die," protested Gloria.

"If we don't, we all die," Slocum said, getting his arm around Benbow and heaving. The man was heavier than he looked. Even with Benbow's feeble efforts to help, Slocum had a devil of a time getting him to his horse. The man would never be able to ride upright; Slocum tossed him belly down over the saddle, and then secured him with lengths of rawhide cut from the gear.

"I think someone's coming," Gloria said uneasily. "From the direction of Road Agent Rock."

Slocum grunted as he swung into the saddle. He sought the outlaw he had wounded, but failed to find the man. It didn't matter if they found him or he survived to tell the others in the gang what had happened. With Henry Plummer free and uninjured, all hell was out for lunch.

Keeping the pace brisk, Slocum forced Gloria to ride hard. She protested that he would kill her brother, but Slocum ignored her. He had to. Plummer might ride on into Bannack and get a posse together to hunt them down. Slocum wanted to find a safe hideout by then.

"Where do we go, John? Samuel needs help soon."

"I'm tracking Plummer. He knows these mountain

passes better than anyone.'' Slocum saw evidence of recent passage. Plummer had come this way and made no effort to hide his headlong flight. The trail would wind around and get them to Bannack. Slocum didn't doubt that. But what would they do in town? Plummer still kept it under his thumb.

"The doctor will help us," Gloria said, as if reading his mind. "The others in town will also. They know what's going on, how big a crook their sheriff really is."

"So?" Slocum was unimpressed. Even if what Gloria said was true—and it probably was—he had a low opinion of most town dwellers. They were sheep being fattened for slaughter. And then only after they had been sheared a few times.

"I can rally them," she said. "They are disgusted with Sheriff Plummer and his thieving ways. They will stop him."

Slocum knew a fairy tale when he heard one. The townspeople would have formed their vigilance committee a long time back if they had been the least bit willing to stop the robberies along the Alder Gulch Road. Slocum suspected Plummer kept the peace in Bannack and appeased the citizens just enough to keep them in line.

"At least the doctor won't turn us away," Slocum said with some confidence. The doctor would patch up Samuel Benbow for a fee. And if he wasn't inclined to do so, Slocum knew the value of a cocked six-shooter pointed at a man's head. It provided real incentive to doing the right thing.

For an hour they rode through the canyons, and suddenly rode out of a rocky notch to find Bannack spread out below them. The trail down to the town was steep but passable, even for a man slung over the back of his horse. From time to time Slocum glanced over at Samuel Benbow and saw the man feebly kicking or trying to get free. It wasn't comfortable for the wounded man, but Slocum knew Benbow would never have made it to the outskirts of town sitting in his saddle.

"There's the doctor's back door," said Gloria, her face flushed. "We must hurry."

Slocum led Benbow's horse to the back door and wrestled the man off. Struggling with the deadweight, Slocum got to the door and kicked hard several times to draw the doctor's attention. The door opened. The doctor's mouth opened, then snapped shut.

"My brother," Gloria blurted out. "He's been shot. Help him!"

"Yes, yes, of course, bring him in," the doctor said, holding the door for Slocum. Samuel Benbow managed to take a few steps on his own, then collapsed on the doctor's table. Slocum noted damp spots on its side. Fresh blood. It had been a busy morning already.

"What happened?" the doctor asked, rolling up his sleeves.

"Hunting accident," Slocum said before Gloria could say a word. She held her brother's hand and whispered encouragingly to him.

Slocum took her arm and steered her away from the surgery. "Let the physician work on him," Slocum said.

"I'll be back, Samuel. You're going to be fine." She dabbed at tears forming in the corners of her eyes, then left. Slocum hesitated, his appraising stare fixed on the doctor. The surgeon bustled about to get his tools ready for their gory job. Then he went out after Gloria.

In the street in front of the doctor's office Slocum saw Bannack was not quite as it had been. A tension filled the town. People fearfully peered out of doorways rather than coming out to follow their business.

"They know," Gloria said firmly. "They know Plummer's reign of terror is ending. I'll go see if I can sway them."

"Do that," Slocum said. He felt uneasy, and thought he

knew the reason. Gloria Benbow rushed away, not asking what bothered Slocum. She might not have noticed how edgy he was. He waited until she turned into the general store to speak with the furtive owner, then circled the doctor's building and waited at the back door.

Slocum didn't wait long. The doctor came out, not looking around until he heard Slocum's Colt cock.

"What is the meaning of this?" the doctor demanded. A slight stammer betrayed his nervousness.

"You finished with your patient already?" Slocum asked, the six-gun in his hand never wavering as it pointed directly at the doctor's face.

"I . . . I need things," the doctor said lamely. He had turned as pale as his patient.

"You see a lot of work this morning? I saw fresh blood on your table."

"Another hunting accident," the doctor said.

"Maybe it was Plummer's deputy. He caught a bullet in his chest."

"Shoulder," the doctor corrected, then instantly knew he had betrayed himself. As Slocum had figured, the doctor was securely in Plummer's hip pocket.

"Get back in there and do your job. I wouldn't take it too kindly if Mr. Benbow upped and died."

"He's seriously wounded. You know that. He might not make it, no matter what I do."

"Be brilliant," Slocum said, motioning for the doctor to get back into his surgery. "Or you might find yourself operating on yourself."

Slocum sat and watched, gun idly dangling in his hand as the doctor sweated, cursed, and worked to pull the lead from Samuel Benbow. Slocum had seen enough gunshot wounds in his day to know the doctor worked as well as any man could. Only when the gauze bandage went over the stitched-up hole did Slocum relax.

"Where were you heading when I stopped you? The sheriff's office?"

The doctor nodded.

"Then you stay here with your patient. You might put your tools back in that little black bag and come on over to the jailhouse in about a half hour."

"Why?"

"I reckon your sheriff's going to need your services then," Slocum said grimly. He shoved his Colt back into his cross-draw holster and left.

It had been a full day and the sun was setting, casting long shadows behind Slocum as he headed for the jail and Sheriff Plummer.

Slocum felt as if the world crushed in on him. Every step he took in Plummer's direction gave him a cold chill. It took several minutes before he figured out why. Bannack's main street was empty of the usual bustle. No one came and went from the saloons. The stores might as well have been shut down for all the business they did. And eyes. Everywhere he turned he saw furtive eyes peering at him from hiding. The instant he locked gazes, the eyes vanished. He might as well have been trying to out-stare a frightened rabbit.

The people of Bannack had gone into their burrows and weren't coming out. They sensed the fight brewing.

Slocum hoped it wouldn't be his body lying in the middle of the street. He remembered too well the deputies backing up Sheriff Plummer. Like the outlaws at Road Agent Rock they carried rifles and shotguns. All Slocum wanted was to face down Henry Plummer.

"Plummer!" he called, stopping in front of the town jail. "I want to talk."

Slocum widened his stance and shifted slightly so the ebony butt of his Colt Navy was free. He made a fist of his right hand, then relaxed. If Plummer showed himself, Slocum was ready to draw.

"What brings you here, Slocum?" said the sheriff's voice from inside the jailhouse. Plummer was playing it cagey. Slocum looked up and down the street to be sure he wasn't being put into a cross fire by the sheriff's men. He saw no one.

"You shot Samuel Benbow and murdered his pa. You been robbing and thieving along Alder Gulch too long. It's time for you to face up to your crimes."

"You calling me out, Slocum?" Plummer laughed. "I'm sheriff. You're nothing but an outlaw. I can have a dozen men testify they saw you out on the Gulch road sticking up a gold shipment."

"They're your gang, Plummer," Slocum said. In a lower voice, he added, "And I know how you've been cheating them too."

"What's that?"

"The gold you're hiding from them. You stash it, then kill off your gang one by one. At the end of the year, you're not going to divide it among them. You intend keeping it all for yourself. And I know where you hid it."

Slocum saw the anger flare on Plummer's face as the sheriff stepped into the doorway. The man's hands twitched and his breathing became hurried. Plummer was spooked and that would make him an easier target.

"I should have gunned you down the minute I laid eyes on you, Slocum."

"Here's your chance to fix what you think's wrong," Slocum said. "Or you can just give it up and let the federal marshal up in Helena take over this fine town. If you co-operate with the marshal, you might not swing for your crimes."

"I'd hang," Plummer said. "There's no way around it, if I ever got to court. But I won't. Bannack is *my* town, and I intend to keep on running it the way I see fit."

Plummer stepped out, his hand steadier now. The anger was forced away, and Slocum had lost his edge against a man who usually had ice water flowing in his veins.

"You ready to die, Slocum?"

Slocum caught his breath when he heard a dozen six-shooters being cocked. Deeper metallic clicks told him of rifles ready to fire. And the unmistakable clunk of a double-barreled shotgun's hammers coming back sounded directly behind him.

What Slocum didn't understand was the expression on Plummer's face. The sheriff's deputies had Slocum covered. From the number of weapons, all of Plummer's deputies were arrayed behind him.

"It's all right, John. They'll take care of Plummer now."

Slocum chanced a quick look over his shoulder. Gloria Benbow stood to one side of the owner of the general store. In the man's hands rested the double-barreled shotgun. And beside him were two clerks, both armed with rifles. And around them were a dozen other townspeople, all armed—and all aiming smack dab at their sheriff.

"Don't go getting yourselves all riled up," called Plummer. "I can handle this owlhoot."

"We got the real owlhoot in our sights, Plummer," said the store owner. "We've had enough of you and your ways."

"Yeah," shouted another. "Why should we have to pay taxes *and* a weekly protection fee to you? You've been robbin' us. And this little lady tells us what we were too scared to put into words. *You* are the one responsible for the robberies along the Gulch road. You've been stealin' in town and out!"

This produced wrathful comments that grew louder. Here and there Slocum heard mumbled threats of a lynching. Gloria came and stood beside him, but Slocum kept his eyes fixed on the sheriff. Henry Plummer wasn't the kind of man to be taken without a fight.

"We already rounded up your deputies," the store owner said. "We have them all trussed up over in the livery. I reckon they're as guilty as you are!''

Another resentful round of mumbled threats passed through the crowd.

''You boys don't know what you're doing,'' Plummer warned.

''We know,'' someone else said. ''And we intend to fetch the marshal from up Helena way and get you to trial for all you done. You kilt my brother-in-law, you slimy bastard!'' The man surged forward, only to be restrained by others.

''This is the Vigilance Committee of Bannack's first official act,'' the shopkeeper said pretentiously. ''We're placin' you under arrest, Henry Plummer, and we'll be waitin' for the circuit judge to ride through.''

''You've got no evidence. And if you listen to the likes of this one,'' he said, pointing at Slocum, ''if you listen to him, then you're listening to an outlaw bigger than I ever could be!''

Those were Plummer's parting words. The vigilantes surged forward and stripped their sheriff of his derringer and other weapons, tossing them into the street. Pushing forward, they got him into his own calaboose.

Slocum watched, and knew he hadn't heard the last of Henry Plummer.

19

"More dead bodies?" John Slocum asked, seeing another freight wagon rattling into town from the direction of the main road. It passed by and went directly to the undertaker's parlor.

"The Vigilance Committee has been digging up every suspicious spot along Alder Gulch Road. They have found more than one hundred bodies," Gloria Benbow said, dabbing at her nose with a handkerchief. "But none has been our father."

"You've looked at every corpse brought in?" Slocum was astounded. He had seen mass killing during the war and it never ceased to sicken him. Some men had grown used to it. Not him. And he doubted Gloria had gotten so inured that the sight of decaying flesh didn't worry like a terrier at her very soul.

"The perfidy of Sheriff Plummer knows no bounds," she said in her almost prim fashion. She was still playing the English lady in town. "Burying his victims was clever. The men simply vanished, or so it seemed. He could even form a posse of locals and ride out in search of the lost victims and never worry about one turning up alive to indict him."

"No witnesses," murmured Slocum. "What of Hunter and Stinson? Have they been caught yet?"

"No, and the Committee is unable to find Road Agent Rock. Even the best trackers have been unable to find Plummer's hideout." She turned blue eyes toward him. "Would you help them find the outlaws' camp? I got so turned around on our way to Bannack I would be of little help to them."

"Reckon they have their hands full," Slocum said, his mind turning to the gold hidden there. Plummer was in jail, but his two henchmen were still on the loose. Slocum didn't put it past either Stinson or Hunter to put the stolen gold onto pack animals and leave their boss in the calaboose. After all, Plummer would have done the same to them had the tables been turned.

"The judge won't be by for another week," Gloria said, "but the townspeople are growing restive. See how they talk among themselves?"

Slocum had grown increasingly wary of the Bannack citizens. They were turning against anyone who didn't call the town home, turning in on themselves and shutting out the world. At the center of that self-absorption burned a festering hatred for Henry Plummer and his men. With the evidence against Plummer growing daily, a lynch mob would form long before the judge arrived.

"How's Samuel doing?" Slocum asked, suddenly changing the subject.

"You want us to leave Bannack before the trial, don't you."

"The town's a powder keg getting ready to blow. Getting back to Coeur d'Alene might be a good idea long about now," he said.

"Plummer's fate is important to both of us, and Samuel is recovering well. He is up and walking a little, though there is a chance he will be unable to use his right arm again."

"Pity," Slocum said, but his mind wasn't on Benbow's injuries but rather on the men responsible for them. Across the street two men dismounted, men Slocum had seen before—in Plummer's camp at Road Agent Rock.

If anyone was going to break Plummer out of jail, now would be the best time. The longer Plummer stayed in his own jailhouse, the less likely it was that his destination would be anywhere other than the town cemetery.

Two Committee members, red scarves tied onto their arms to set them apart, swaggered down the middle of the street. Both carried sawed-off shotguns capable of reducing a man to a pile of bloody ribbons in an instant. The careless way they swung those weapons about told Slocum they were looking for any excuse to use them.

It was always this way. When timid men got a taste of power, they didn't know when to stop throwing their weight around. Sheep might band together to kick a wolf to death, but the flock never went on to attack their shepherd. In some ways, Slocum wished townspeople were more like sheep.

"I'm leaving in the morning," Slocum said. The sun edged down over the distant rim of the mountains.

"Perhaps you are right, John. You have a good head for such things. We might be overstaying our welcome in Bannack." She turned her lovely face up to him. If they hadn't been in public he would have kissed her.

"If you ride on out too, I can go with you," he said. But Gloria shook her head vigorously. He had not expected anything less from her.

"The trial. We *must* see justice done. Henry Plummer

will not escape judgment this time.''

''How do you bring a man enough justice who has murdered a hundred or more?'' Slocum inclined his head in the direction of the wagon where vigilantes worked to unload four rotting corpses. ''How do you get enough justice for Plummer to avenge even your pa's death?''

''He won't do it anymore. That has to be enough,'' Gloria said, but Slocum knew it wasn't. In some ways, Gloria was like him. She was regretting not killing Plummer herself when she had the chance.

''Why don't you go see how your brother is doing?'' Slocum suggested. He watched the two riders across the street. They made their way down a twilight-darkened alley and around behind the saloon. From what he could tell, several men left the saloon, using the back door. Something was in the wind and Slocum thought he knew what it was.

He glanced after the strutting Committee members making their way down the middle of the street, and knew telling them would do no good. In their way, they were as cowardly now as they had ever been. Given power, they were brutal. Put in jeopardy, they would fold like a bad poker hand.

''Very well, John. You seem distracted. Are you all right?''

''Planning my trip out, that's all,'' he said, knowing his departure from Bannack might come sooner than morning.

''Take care of yourself, John.'' Gloria hesitated, then said in a low voice so no one could overhear, ''Come by my room at the hotel later. For a proper farewell.''

Slocum nodded, knowing it probably would not happen. Gloria gave him a tentative smile, then turned and walked away. Only then did he check his Colt to be sure it was loaded and ready for action. Even before Gloria went into the doctor's office, Slocum was across the street and heading down the alley after the road agents he had spotted.

Four men stood in a tight knot at the far end of the alley,

arguing. Slocum pressed back against a splintery wall, try-ing to get the drift of their dispute. For all their gesturing, they spoke in tones too low for him to hear.

Then they pulled up bandannas over their faces and drew their six-guns. Slocum had been right. These were Plummer's men come to rescue him.

They made their way to the alley beside the jail. One jumped up and spoke quickly to a prisoner inside. For the first time Slocum overheard the exchange. Buck Stinson had come for his boss, and Plummer was both relieved and angry it had taken his lieutenant this long to get up the nerve to break him out of jail.

Slocum walked into the street and waited for the men to rush into the jail. They quickly overcame the vigilantes posted there as jailers. Four outlaws had gone in. Five emerged, Henry Plummer strapping on a six-shooter as he left the jail.

"Last time they took you away before we finished, Plummer," Slocum called. "Not this time."

Henry Plummer went for his gun at the first words from Slocum's lips. But Slocum was also drawing. His hand was a blur as it closed around the butt of his Colt Navy. He drew and fanned off four fast shots. All four found targets, two in Plummer and one each in Stinson and another of the former sheriff's henchmen.

Slocum had winged them, but not fatally. Plummer and the others yelped in pain and returned fire. The blistering hail of lead drove Slocum to the ground. He got off two more shots, killing the one he thought was Buck Stinson.

Then Slocum's hammer fell on an empty chamber.

"Come on, Boss. We gotta get out of here." This had to be Bill Hunter urging his leader to escape. But Plummer would have none of it.

"I have unfinished business," Plummer said coldly. He leveled his six-shooter at Slocum and started to pull the trigger. A single shot rang out. Plummer grunted and clutched his gun hand. The bullet had bored cleanly through his wrist, causing his six-gun to drop from limp fingers.

Not to be cheated, Plummer dropped to his knees and fumbled for his fallen six-shooter with his left hand. Another shot knocked him to the ground. But the former lawman was still alive and struggling.

Slocum turned and saw his benefactor was none other than Gloria Benbow. She knocked open her derringer and worked to reload. It would be too late. Those with Plummer were turning their smoking pistols in her direction—and Slocum's Colt was empty.

"Gloria, get down!" he cried. Slocum tried to get to his feet, but a bullet tore off the heel of his boot, knocking him back to the dusty street.

Gloria Benbow calmly closed her derringer and fired twice more in Plummer's direction. Slocum didn't know if either bullet hit the sheriff. From all around came more gunfire than he could remember since Gettysburg. The reports didn't come in waves as some exhausted their ammunition and others took up the firing. It came in a continuous assault on his ears, more like an explosion than individual guns firing.

As quickly as it had come, the onslaught ended. Vigilance Committee members appeared as if by magic. In threes and fours they came until they surrounded Henry Plummer and his gang members.

"The varmints are still alive," protested one vigilante.

"Let's do something about that," cried another. A weakly struggling Henry Plummer was pulled to his feet. Bill Hunter joined him. Buck Stinson had died from Slocum's bullets; the vigilantes hoisted him up too. The two remaining would-be rescuers were herded along, prodded by rifle barrels toward the edge of town.

"Wait, no!" cried Gloria Benbow. "You can't do this."

"You want to save him for the trial?" asked Slocum.

"I want to kill the son of a bitch!" cried Gloria. "I

thought about all you said. *I* want to kill him with my own hand!''

Slocum grabbed her slender wrist and forced the derringer away. She could only wound or kill one of the vigilantes surrounding Plummer.

"They have blood in their eyes," Slocum warned. "They'll string up the lot of them." He snorted in disgust. He understood Gloria's feelings and shared them. He had wanted to end Plummer's miserable life himself for all the outlaw sheriff had done to him.

Slocum and Gloria Benbow followed the crowd to the town limits and found bodies already swaying gently in the evening breeze. Henry Plummer and his cronies had come to the end of their ropes on the limb of a huge oak tree. The Vigilance Committee had even hanged Stinson, in spite of him being dead.

"Samuel will not be pleased," Gloria said without any remorse in her voice. "He would have wanted to put the noose around Plummer's neck himself. Now, neither of us will have the pleasure of ending his foul life!"

With that she turned and walked away. Slocum knew he would ignore her invitation to go to her hotel room later that night.

Slocum threw the saddle over the back of his horse and cinched the belly strap tight. He turned at the sound of someone approaching.

"John, I missed you last night," Gloria said softly. She stood outlined by the sun peeking up over the mountains around Bannack. It made her look more like an angel than the devil who had wanted to take her father's killer's life with her own hands.

"I don't think so," he told her truthfully. "Neither of us was in much of a mood for that."

"Perhaps so. Samuel and I are going on to Coeur d'Alene. I have a wagon rented so he can ride in the bed."

"That's good," Slocum said.

"John, come with us. Please." She clutched his arm with feverish intensity.

"Don't know it would work out, Gloria," he told her.

"You might be right about that too, John," she said. "You might also be wrong. Let's find out."

He shook his head. He wasn't cut out to be tied down, even with a filly as good-looking, intelligent, and willing as Gloria Benbow.

"Then it's good-bye," she said, giving him a quick peck on the cheek that didn't satisfy either of them. She stepped back a pace, flashed him her wicked smile that excited him so, and added, "I just spoke with the federal marshal from Helena."

"Don't reckon he's too happy about the lynching yesterday," Slocum said.

"He doesn't care. If anything, it makes his life easier. No, I asked him something else."

Slocum waited. Her blue eyes twinkled.

"They haven't found Road Agent Rock yet—nor any of the gold Plummer stole over the past year."

Slocum nodded slightly. He might come out ahead yet. He had a good notion where Plummer might have hidden his gold away from the others in his gang. The outlaws would have hightailed it as soon as they heard their leader had been put into jail. Only the two outlaws with Hunter and Stinson had remained loyal, Slocum suspected. And they were dead, their necks an inch or two longer than before.

"There's a present from Samuel and me," Gloria went on. She pointed to three mules, already outfitted with packs. Empty packs. Packs waiting for several hundred pounds of gold to be stashed in them.

Slocum looked at her appraisingly and finally said, "If I find it, there's no reason my trail can't wind through Coeur d'Alene. For a little while."

"I'll be waiting for you, John Slocum," Gloria said. This time she gave him a proper kiss and ran from the stable.

Slocum gathered the lead mule's reins and then mounted his horse, riding slowly from Bannack and heading into the mountains. The gold might not be there. But he thought it was. And sharing it with Gloria and her brother seemed only fair after all they had been through together.

Only fair indeed.

JAKE LOGAN

TODAY'S HOTTEST ACTION WESTERN!

TOP WESTERN TITLES
FROM JOVE BOOKS!

__HIGH MOUNTAIN WINTER
   by Frances Hurst   0-515-11825-7/$5.99

It was 1850, and a young nation looked westward to the promise of new land and a new life. But Maryla Stoner's destiny takes a different turn when her family dies on the journey west and Maryla must survive the high mountain winter...alone. Based on a true story.

__ME AND THE BOYS
   by Ellen Recknor   0-515-11698-X/$5.99

Sixteen-year-old Gini Kincaid had hair of flame and a spirit to match. Running with outlaws, her name was on the tongues of righteous and criminal folk across the Southwest. And she had a mouth that got her into all kinds of trouble...

__THUNDER IN THE VALLEY
   by Jim R. Woolard   0-515-11630-0/$4.99

Falsely accused of trading with Indians, Matthan Hannar barely escaped the hangman's noose. He ran for his life through the treacherous valley, eluding scalpers and surviving the wilderness. Now, for the sake of a woman, he was going back...where the noose was waiting for him.